NEWS

When we got into the airlock, we could see through its inner window that another man was waiting with the lock attendant; as soon as the pressure equalized and we got the doors open, he came forward. It was Paul.

I knew something was wrong just from his voice—it was his minister's voice, not that of the friend I'd laughed and joked with so often. He took my arm and led me into the crowded little Ground Control office. "Melinda," Paul said, "I don't know any way to tell you this except directly. There's been an accident. . . ."

FIREBIRD
WHERE SCIENCE FICTION SOARS™

JOURNEY
BETWEEN WORLDS

Sylvia Engdahl

DECORATIONS BY
James and Ruth McCrea

FIREBIRD
AN IMPRINT OF PENGUIN GROUP (USA) INC.

Western Star by Stephen Vincent Benét, Holt, Rinehart and Winston, Inc. Copyright ©
1943 by Rosemary Carr Benet. Reprinted by permission of Brandt & Brandt. "Desert
Places" from *Complete Poems of Robert Frost*. Copyright © 1936 by Robert Frost.
Copyright © 1964 by Lesley Frost Ballantine. Reprinted by permission of Holt, Rinehart
and Winston, Inc. "Wanderin' Star" copyright © 1952 by Alan Jay Lerner. Reprinted by
permission of Margot Johnson Agency.

FIREBIRD
Published by the Penguin Group
Penguin Group (USA) Inc., 345 Hudson Street, New York, New York 10014, U.S.A.
Penguin Group (Canada), 90 Eglinton Avenue East, Suite 700,
Toronto, Ontario, Canada M4P 2Y3 (a division of Pearson Penguin Canada Inc.)
Penguin Books Ltd, 80 Strand, London WC2R 0RL, England
Penguin Ireland, 25 St Stephen's Green, Dublin 2, Ireland
(a division of Penguin Books Ltd)
Penguin Group (Australia), 250 Camberwell Road, Camberwell,
Victoria 3124, Australia (a division of Pearson Australia Group Pty Ltd)
Penguin Books India Pvt Ltd, 11 Community Centre,
Panchsheel Park, New Delhi - 110 017, India
Penguin Group (NZ), 67 Apollo Drive, Mairangi Bay, Auckland 1311, New Zealand
(a division of Pearson New Zealand Ltd)
Penguin Books (South Africa) (Pty) Ltd, 24 Sturdee Avenue,
Rosebank, Johannesburg 2196, South Africa

First published in hardcover in the United States of America by Atheneum, 1970
Reissued by G. P. Putnam's Sons, a division of Penguin Young Readers Group, 2006
Published by Firebird, an imprint of Penguin Group (USA) Inc., 2007

1 3 5 7 9 10 8 6 4 2

Text copyright © Sylvia Louise Engdahl, 1970, 2006
All rights reserved

THE LIBRARY OF CONGRESS HAS CATALOGED THE G. P. PUTNAM'S SONS EDITION AS FOLLOWS:
Engdahl, Sylvia Louise. Journey between worlds / Sylvia Louise Engdahl ;
decorations by James and Ruth McCrea.—1st G.P. Putnam's Sons ed.   p. cm.
Summary: To prove her independence to her boyfriend, Melinda decides to go to Mars
on a pleasure trip—an impromptu decision that changes her entire way of life.
ISBN 0-399-24532-7 (hc)
[1. Science Fiction.] I. McCrea, James, ill. II. McCrea, Ruth, ill. III. Title.
PZ7.E6985Jo 2006 [Fic]—dc22 2005030932
ISBN 978-0-14-240828-5
Printed in the United States of America

Contents

Part One
EARTH

Chapter 1

I never wanted to go to Mars. So many girls plan to be flight attendants, or ship's technicians, or if they're going to get a degree, they hope to land a position in the Colonies just as soon as they can qualify; and not only because of the fabulous salaries. I was never like that. In our senior year, we used to talk about college and jobs, and all the things we wanted to do with our lives—though of course we knew that for most of us, Europe or Africa or maybe Tahiti would be the extent of our travels. Even then, what I wanted was to live in a house overlooking the bay, with the sparkling blue water in front and dark trees behind, near the town where my mother's folks had always lived. And since teaching was a career that would let me do that, I did not intend to let anything stand in the way of getting my Oregon teaching credentials as soon as I possibly could.

Yet here I am in New Terra. There are times when I still can't believe it.

Sometimes I dream about the water lapping on the rocks below Gran's beach house. Or the sand, white instead of red and damp where the tide has left it, and the breeze smelling of salt and seaweed and free oxygen. And the firs, ragged green against a pale blue sky, and white clouds billowing up behind the mountains . . . or fog. Fog, soft and wet against my face, and indoors, the comforting fragrance of a crackling wood fire.

Then when I wake up and first remember how far away those things are, I don't see how I can bear it. And I lie there thinking about all that's happened, and wondering whether making a trip to Mars was very foolish of me or very mature. You can't ever plan everything out in advance, I guess. But I used to think I could. I don't think I wanted too much; the trouble was, I didn't want enough.

Mostly, I wanted to marry Ross. We had been dating for over two years by the time of my graduation from high school, and for most of that time we had considered ourselves in love. Ross's parents liked me; I had been to their home for dinner frequently, and I had spent several school vacations with them. Ross's dad was an attorney, as Ross was to be, and very successful; but I never pictured myself as the same sort of wife as Ross's mother. I was terribly shy, and the thought of giving all those parties and entertaining important clients appalled me. Ross laughed at me, but he didn't really care. He said he would be happy to live in the homey old Maple Beach house, which was Gran's and would someday be mine, especially since it was less than a hundred miles commuting distance to Portland.

We'd discussed getting married after our freshman year of college, though I hadn't mentioned that either to Gran or to Dad. They knew I was dating Ross, but families—especially parents whom one doesn't see often—don't quite take in the fact that boys and girls in school can be seriously in love. Several of my friends made the mistake of insisting that their folks acknowledge their love as real and lasting; all it got them was quarrels and unhappiness. Not that the girls in my crowd wanted to quit school for the sake of marriage, or anything like that. It's simply that you seem more like an adult if other adults agree that you are old enough to make final decisions about things. Nobody knows this better than parents, and parents don't want to think of their kids as adults. This is less because they distrust you than because they distrust themselves; it's a matter not of your age, but of theirs. They hate to believe that they are old enough to have grown children. So if you love your folks, why make it tough for them? I adored Dad; when I wrote to him I told him only that Ross was fun to date and that we liked each other a lot. If there was more in our relationship, well, it was nothing that wasn't perfectly decent and natural. I never felt that I was hiding anything.

So Dad thought that I would be thrilled at the prospect of taking time out for a long trip before I started college.

I'd better explain about Dad. First of all let me say that he was a wonderful person, the nicest father any girl was ever lucky enough to have. Really. The only trouble was, I never saw enough of him. When my mother died I was only nine and Dad was doing on-site engineering for a firm under government contract, which meant a transfer halfway around the world every six months or so; of course he couldn't take me along. I was sent to live with my great-grandmother, Mother's grandmother, and that was when I got to love Maple Beach so much. I had always lived in city apartments before and this was like a whole new world for me, even if Gran was somewhat strict and old-fashioned. But I missed Dad. I used to count the hours when I knew he'd be coming for a visit. The visits were all too rare; he was in Melbourne that year.

Later, when I went away to school, I was lonesome not only for Dad but for the beach house, and my collies, and most of all, for Gran herself. I hope I haven't given the impression that I didn't love my great-grandmother. She was—well, reserved, I suppose you'd call it, but she was kind, too. And she gave me roots. Western Oregon had been home to Gran's people for generations, ever since the pioneer days. (Gran had a gold locket, very worn, that one of her ancestors—Melinda Stillwell, the one I'm named after—had been given the day she set out to cross the plains in a covered wagon. I can remember sitting on a corner of the stair landing with Gran's green leather jewel box between my knees, swinging that locket by its dull chain and wondering what it would be like to come to a place that was just wilderness.) The Maple Beach house had been built by that first Melinda's great-grandson about the time of the World Wars, I'm never sure which one. It was a terribly old-fashioned house, built mostly of wood with obsolete glass windows, but Gran loved it. It was her home, and in my imagination it was mine, too, though it wasn't really, for I lived there only three years.

To get back to Dad. He'd always promised that once I was through school we'd spend some time together, a whole summer, maybe. He was going to show me all of Europe if he could arrange a transfer there at the right moment; or failing that, we would visit some of the most historic spots on weekends. At any rate, we'd really get to know each other, the way we hadn't when I was a child. "Before it's too late," he used to tell me. "Before you're grown up and on your own." Though I didn't want to leave Maple Beach or Ross for very long, I was happy about it. I expected to major in history at college, so seeing Europe would be useful; yet it wasn't so much that as the idea of being with Dad at last.

You know, much as I loved Dad, I never stopped to think that he might not be completely happy. He hadn't remarried after my mother's death and from his letters I always assumed that his work was everything to him. He had a top position; he was an executive by the time I entered boarding school, and was making loads of money. I didn't realize how much he missed not having a family. Moreover, it just never occurred to me that there might be something else he'd always wanted that he'd never had a chance for. I didn't find out about it until the day of my graduation. If I hadn't been so absorbed with Ross, maybe it wouldn't have been such a shock.

Though I don't know. How would you feel if your father gave you a ticket to Mars for a graduation present?

I had absolutely no advance warning. As late as that last day at school, I wasn't sure if we were taking a trip at all. I hadn't seen Dad since Christmas, when I had joined him in Washington, D.C., because Dad's current work was in his firm's home office, and he hadn't been able to come to the West Coast for even a few days. In his letters he hadn't given an inkling as to where his next assignment might take him. He hadn't mentioned summer, except to say that he was looking forward to having me with him. It was exasperating. I don't like surprises; I like to have everything mapped out, and it seemed as if Dad should have known that. (Though come to think of it, he really knew very little about me—my personality, I mean—since he hadn't seen me often enough.) As it was, I didn't know if I'd be two days at Gran's or a month before Dad would want me to join him. I didn't even know if he was coming to graduation.

I was depressed that day to begin with, for several reasons. It wasn't only the uncertainty. First, Gran had phoned; she'd come down with a bad cold and wasn't going to be able to make it out to school for the ceremonies, so if Dad didn't show up, I'd have no one at all. Ross's parents would be there, but somehow it isn't the same.

Also, now that the time had come, I was beginning to hate the idea of leaving school. I'd been homesick when I first came from Gran's, but that hadn't lasted, and school had been the center of things for six years. I wanted to graduate, but in some ways it was sad and a little scary. After all, I'd have all the rest of my life to live at Maple Beach, after college. Things were changing too fast.

I've often wondered what it would be like to go to school and live at home at the same time. You wouldn't get so wrapped up in it, maybe; graduation wouldn't seem so—so final. Some things would stay the same. It's not that I regret having gone to

Evergreen Central. A residential school was the only choice for me in any case, since there wasn't regular copter service to Gran's house, or even a bus. But I'm sure I wouldn't have liked a city high school. No trees, no lawns, not even gym outdoors! If you're not underground, you might just as well be. And think of the hours some kids devote to commuting. Dad's folks were English, so it seemed more natural to him for me to live at school than it did to Gran. When she was a girl the only boarding schools were private ones, and she never has understood about tax-supported residential schools being the new trend.

Lots of kids like residential schools just because there's less fighting with their parents. Dorm counselors may be a little overbearing at times, but from what I've heard they have a better understanding of your problems than the average parent has. I wouldn't know; I've always wished I could have been close to Dad and Mother, yet if I'd seen them every day we might not have gotten along. The thing I do know, though, is that it's easier to make friends at a residential school. You meet kids from all over, not just those from your own suburb; and even if you're not the kind to go out for activities much, there are always your roommates. I wouldn't have met Julie Tamura or Lorene Smith at a local school, and we turned out to be best friends. Of course, if we hadn't just naturally liked one another, sharing a room might have been worse than being lonely. I admit I've always found it hard to get on intimate terms with people. Especially with boys. I hate to think what it would have been like if I hadn't had Ross.

If it hadn't been for Ross, I would have looked forward to college with a certain amount of apprehension, I think. Neither Julie nor Lorene was going to the University of Oregon. But Ross would be there, which was why I'd chosen it; we'd spend all our free time together. It really wasn't going to matter, not knowing anyone else. To get my teaching credentials in minimum time I'd have to study hard; the first year would go fast. And after that we'd be married.

Only, this summer we were going to be separated. That was another thing that depressed me on graduation day. Because the night before, while we were walking back from the coffee shop, Ross had brought it up again, and the evening hadn't ended happily. It wasn't exactly a fight—Ross and I never fought, because I almost always saw things his way—but it certainly didn't put me in a mood to enjoy graduation. The trouble was, Ross had never been really resigned to my spending the summer with Dad.

"Can't you get out of going?" he'd complained. It wasn't the first time he had asked that, either.

"You know I can't. You know I don't want to. Do we have to go through it all again?"

"If you loved me you'd want to."

"You're not being fair, Ross. Of course I love you. But can't I love my own father, too?"

"What am I supposed to do all summer while you're gone?"

"I thought you were going to work."

"I don't mean that."

I said slowly, "If you want to date, you can." I didn't think he'd take me seriously, and naturally he didn't; neither of us had dated anyone else for more than a year. But he didn't laugh it off, either. He didn't say a word until we got back to the dorm, and I finally had to try to fix things up myself.

"Oh, Ross, we'll never be separated again," I said. "I promise we won't. It's just that I've wanted to see more of Dad for so long, and I'll never have another chance."

"Sure, Mel. Go ahead, have your trip. See you in the fall."

For a moment I thought he meant not until fall. "I'll see you tomorrow, won't I? At lunch? And after—"

"Of course. Unless you'd rather go out with your father than with me."

"On Grad Night? Don't be ridiculous." I refrained from saying that Dad might not even be coming. Ross and I had been planning our Grad Night date for a long time; we were going into Portland. Ross would drive me out to Gran's house later, whether Dad showed up or not. "It may be the last date we'll have for a long time," I reminded him. "Please don't spoil it."

"Well, there's nothing left to argue about, is there? It's settled; you're going." He smiled then, and his kiss was the same as always.

It never occurred to either one of us that *where* I was going would make any difference. But it did; it brought on the only real fight we ever had. And if it hadn't been for that fight with Ross, I might never have come to Mars at all. It's funny the way things happen.

Graduation day was gorgeous, lush and green as only a terrestrial June can be. I remember everything about that afternoon:

the way the clouds looked, and how the sun broke through and shone warm on my shoulders, and threw soft shadows across the stone floor of the quadrangle. The rhododendrons were in bloom, brilliant pink against the green mass of the maples. I always loved the rhododendrons.

Dad arrived less than half an hour before the ceremonies, on the fifteen-forty copter. We'd had the morning free for getting our things together and clearing up details like returning discs to the library, so by fifteen o'clock I'd finished packing. Julie and I had our caps and gowns on and were sitting in the quad near the fountain, just outside the entrance to the auditorium where the line was to form. I was miserably nervous; if only Dad had told me, one way or the other. Since he hadn't, I'd keep hoping right up to the last moment, no matter how hard I tried not to.

From where we sat we could see the school copter busily ferrying people in from the parking compound—it was running every five minutes instead of keeping to the regular schedule—but we couldn't see who was getting off. We would have gone over to the copter pad if it were not that students had been told to keep away because of the crowds; arriving parents were being directed over to the quad. Julie's folks hadn't come yet, either, but they were local people and would be arriving on the monorail instead of driving in from the airport.

The stereo system had been shut off temporarily and we could hear the school band tuning up somewhere in the background. The fountain splashed noisily off to our left. (I marvel, now, at the amount of water used in fountains on Earth!) I twisted my hands in my lap and wished that sixteen o'clock would hurry up and come.

"Where's Ross?" Julie asked.

"Oh, meeting his folks, I guess. He said they might not see me until afterward." This should be a happy, exciting time, I was thinking; instead, it was flat and empty. Perhaps the evening would be flat, too. I could hardly wait until it was over and I was on my way out to Maple Beach.

Just as the loudspeakers came on and told us to start lining up, Julie spotted her parents. I was left standing there, knowing that it was foolish to wait any longer. Even if Dad did come, I couldn't talk to him until after it was over; the band was already starting on the introduction to the march.

But when he came rushing down the steps from the copter pad, I forgot everything except what a joy it was to see him, and it didn't matter if I ever went inside for the ceremonies or not.

The first thing I noticed was how excited he seemed, and how happy. Dad grabbed my hands and then hugged me tight, almost smashing my mortarboard, and I began to think I'd been silly to wonder if he cared anything about my graduation. Of course he cared. He was positively ecstatic!

Then he thrust the long white envelope into my hands. From that point on, everything I'd ever known or felt or believed in began to come apart.

"Mel, honey," Dad said. "It's all settled! They're sending you. I didn't tell you because I wasn't sure; I was so afraid you'd be disappointed—"

"Sending me where?" I began, but just then the band burst out with the main chorus of the march from *Aida* and the line started to move.

"Happy graduation, honey!" Dad shouted, and he disappeared in the mob of people pouring in through the now-closing doors. I had to run to find my place in line, and by that time we were already moving into the auditorium. I started to stick the envelope away under the white folds of my gown, but as I did it I caught sight of the imprint in its top left-hand corner.

Whenever I hear *Aida*, I'll close my eyes and I'll see that envelope again, just the way it was as I first looked at it. The triple globes—blue, white, and red—and the tall blue lettering, *Three Planets Corporation.* The triple globes as I'd seen them a thousand times on billboards and in magazines and on TV: blue for Earth, white for the Moon, and red for Mars. The words slanted in blue script across the front of the envelope: SPACELINER RESER- VATIONS. The precise computer-printed characters on the ticket inside, confirming that Melinda Ashley held Berth 2, Cabin G-11, in the S.S. *Susan Constant,* departing at 0415 Greenwich mean time on June 10 for the planet Mars.

I didn't hear one word of the graduation speeches. The thrill you're supposed to get from such a solemn occasion bypassed me completely.

Dad, Dad, I thought that day, *you must know me better than this. You must know this isn't necessary, that I don't even want it. That there isn't anything I want less!* I knew very little about Mars at the time, but I had a general idea of what that ticket must have cost; even for a man who's well-to-do, interplanetary fares are out of sight. I appreciated Dad's wanting to give me a really supercolossal graduation gift to make up for all those years. But I didn't want a trip to Mars, I wanted to be with *him*.

What I didn't know yet was that Dad had just received an assignment from his firm to investigate the feasibility of their opening a branch office on Mars.

Chapter 2

I still don't like to think about graduation day. I still hate to relive that evening, the first evening that I knew we were going to Mars.

What surprised me most was that Dad was so happy about it. We sat on one of the benches in the quad and talked while I was waiting for Ross to get his car packed. (I'd explained about our date, when Dad wanted to take me out for something to eat.) I held the ticket envelope next to my diploma, my damp fingers making a soiled blotch over the triple globes.

"Aren't you excited, honey?" Dad demanded.

Excited wasn't the word for it. Flabbergasted would have been closer. But I was trying to act calm while I got up courage to tell Dad that I'd rather not go to Mars at all.

It wasn't that I was afraid to go. I wouldn't want anyone to get that idea. Or maybe I was and didn't know it; but if so it wasn't physical fear, not then. I had as matter-of-fact an attitude toward space travel as most people have, though I had no personal interest in it, not being the scientific type. But going to Mars is not like going to Europe. For one thing, you're gone longer. At the very least, I would miss two or three terms of college. For another, a different planet is so—well, so foreign.

Not that I was thinking about those drawbacks then. I was thinking about Ross. Perhaps, after all, it had been wrong not to have told Dad long ago how I felt about Ross. Since I hadn't, though, it seemed wisest to bring up the educational angle first.

"Dad," I began, "what about the university? I've been admitted; I'm supposed to start in September."

Dad smiled. "It won't hurt anything for you to wait, Melinda. You'll learn more from a trip to the Colonies than from a year at school in any case, but if you want to forge ahead for your freshman exams, you can study on the ship. There won't be much else to do en route, you know."

I was silent. I had never encountered anyone who'd gone on a spaceship as a fare-paying passenger instead of as a crew member. There aren't many such people, except for the homesteaders, whose fare is paid by the government and whose passage is strictly one way. Dad explained that I'd been right in thinking he couldn't afford the fare. His company was paying it. If my mother had been living she would have been entitled to accompany him, and since she wasn't, he'd talked them into sending me in her place.

"The firm's anxious to get someone from the home office out there right now," he told me. "Someone who'll be back here by next year, when the government appropriation for the Colonies comes up for review again. There's going to be a lot of public discussion about the value of Mars, and it will be a good thing for at least one of our managers to have some firsthand knowledge of the situation."

I tried another tack. "But why do they need you for this job, Dad? Aren't there other men who'd be willing to go?" I'd always had the impression that Dad was enough of a key man in the organization to have pretty much the last word about his assignments.

He laughed. "I outrank them, Mel. I've waited years for this opportunity, and at last I'm high enough up in the firm to have first crack at it." He sounded as pleased as if he had just been elected president of something.

"You—you chose the assignment yourself?"

"Well, I made the right people aware of how I'd feel if I were offered it."

"Dad, what do you mean, you've waited years? I never knew—"

"That I planned to emigrate to the Colonies once?"

"To homestead—you?"

"It was all settled. Our application had been accepted, conditional on our passing the medical exam. Then your mother . . . well, that was when they discovered the heart condition, Mel. We had to give it up."

"My *mother* wanted to go to Mars?" *Why*, I thought, *I would have gone, too. I would have been a Martian.*

"She did, very much. It was in her blood, she said; her ancestors were pioneers." He sighed. "That was a long time ago. When she died I was over the age limit for a nonresident job, and, of course, I wouldn't have wanted to homestead without her even if single immigrants had been allowed. But later, I began to hope that I could go for a trip someday. I've been lucky, Mel; it's worked out."

I don't think he noticed how quiet I was. He tightened his arm around my shoulders and grinned at me. "It was a close thing. I was so afraid I wouldn't be able to fix it so you could come along. Mel, honey, what if I'd had to choose between going to Mars and having you with me?"

What could I say? It just goes to show how two people can have the closest possible family relationship and still not know anything about each other at all. I had never dreamed that Dad was the kind to have any interest in other planets, and he apparently was assuming that because he wanted to go so much, I must feel the same way. And I couldn't blame him. What had I ever done to give him any other idea? When had I ever put any of my real thoughts and feelings into a letter? I had written reams of the casual, newsy stuff that it seemed a father would want to hear. But, it suddenly occurred to me, he hadn't been the only one who'd failed to give much thought to what the person on the other side of the correspondence truly cared about.

I'd gotten into a fine fix! Because I couldn't go, I just couldn't. Why, I'd lose almost a whole year out of my life, and I knew that Ross would be furious. It would upset everything, all the neatly planned steps leading up to the safe, permanent future that I had dreamed about for so long. Ross might not wait a year. If I wasn't with him at the university, he might start dating someone else. He might change his mind about the wedding, want to put it off. He might develop different ideas, so that by the time we were married he might not be willing to live at Maple Beach any-more.

And what use would there be in it? I was an old-fashioned girl at heart; all this space business had always seemed pretty pointless to me. What was wrong with Earth, for goodness sake? The things that were significant, all of history in fact, had happened right there. That first Melinda—the one who'd come as a settler to the Oregon Country and worked so hard to make a home—what would she have thought of people turning their backs on everything that was *natural*?

I wanted to be with Dad, but not enough to risk everything for the sake of a trip I wouldn't even enjoy. Not after the way I'd laughed at girls who would do just about anything to get on board a ship, though I knew they'd be envious. Yet I didn't want to hurt Dad's feelings. He'd tried so hard to arrange my passage that I couldn't come right out and tell him to give the ticket back. I'd have to think of something, but it could wait until tomorrow. Tomorrow we would be at Gran's and I could walk on the beach for a while and think; that was bound to be a help.

I didn't mean to tell Ross that night, and sometimes I wonder how things would have turned out if I hadn't. It just slipped out, really. We were in the car, on our way to Portland. Ross couldn't help but notice that I wasn't being the best of company; in fact I just wasn't responding to him at all.

Ross swung around the last curve of the road from school, eased into the expressway traffic pattern, and put the car on automatic. Then he folded back the wheel and pulled me over to him. We were in the 120 klicks-per-hour lane; there'd been no free slots in the faster ones, so it was going to be a long drive.

After a while he said, "What's the matter, Mel? This is Grad Night, remember? What goes?"

"Nothing. I'm tired, that's all," I lied.

"I thought you'd be happy now that your dad's showed up."

"I was glad to see him, of course."

"Did he say where he's taking you this summer?"

"Please let's not talk about it, Ross."

"Hey, I wasn't going to argue. I promised, didn't I?"

I realized that since Dad was going to Mars and I didn't intend to go with him, Ross and I wouldn't be separated after all. He could come out to Gran's whenever he wanted to. I was anxious to please him by telling him so, I guess, or maybe I thought he'd help me to deal with the problem of Dad. Maybe in the back of my mind was the thought that he just might be willing to move the wedding up to this summer, and would talk to Dad about it himself. At any rate I broke the news. I said, "There's been a change of plans. Dad wants me to go to Mars with him."

Ross took his arm away and stared at me. "You're kidding."

"No, I'm not. He's really going to Mars."

"Even if he is, you don't expect me to believe he'd drag you along. What are you trying to do to me, Mel?"

I drew back, surprised. Ross hadn't been at all like himself over the whole business of my leaving him for the summer, but surely he knew I wasn't the kind of girl who'd tease him deliberately. Did he think I was making it up so that he'd beg me not to go?

"It's true," I said. "If you don't believe me look at my ticket." I pulled it out of my purse and shoved it at him.

Ross examined it carefully, even reading the fine print on the back. Then he laughed. "You're not going to use this, are you?"

"No, of course not."

"Your father sure has his nerve. He's hardly talked to you all this time, and now he expects to snatch you up and take you off to some strange planet fifty million miles away."

That was the wrong thing to say, and Ross should have known better. I mean, how did he expect me to react? As a matter of fact I'd been thinking something along those general lines myself; but what I said was, "You've got it all wrong, Ross. Dad's trying to do something wonderful for me. It's a graduation present."

"Doesn't he care how you feel about it? Why, Mel, you could get killed!"

"Oh, I don't think so, Ross. It's not an especially dangerous trip; I'd be on a regular scheduled spaceliner. *He's* going."

A new thought struck me, though: What if something should happen to Dad? What if we never saw each other again? I'd have missed such a lot; and besides, for a moment I heard him saying, *Mel, honey, what if I'd had to choose. . . .* It dawned on me that he did want me with him very much, and I was forcing a choice on him after all. Two chances that would never come again, this trip he'd always hoped for—a big step in his career probably—against the last time to get acquainted with me as a daughter before I got tied down by college and a job.

"Dad does care," I insisted. "It's just like I told you before, only this Martian assignment came up, and—well, I guess he thought I'd be even more thrilled than if we went to Europe or something."

"Thrilled? Mel, you don't want to go cruising around in space."

I couldn't recall having mentioned to Ross that I didn't. "Some people," I said stiffly, "would call it a once-in-a-lifetime opportunity."

"Well, you're a normal, levelheaded person and the only opportunities you need are right here on Earth."

I don't know why this made me so mad, because it certainly wasn't something I disagreed with. It was just the way he said it, as if I were four years old and had to be educated for my own good. I *was* tired, and had had just about all the strain I could take for one day. So I came right back at him. "Who are you, Ross Franklin, to tell me what opportunities I need?"

"I guess someone has to tell you, if you can even consider anything so stupid."

"What's stupid?"

"Well, the Martian colonies in the first place, for one thing. All the money that's been poured into that piece of barren rock, all the lives lost—it's useless."

Dad and Mother couldn't have thought it entirely useless, I thought, if they had really planned to homestead. And I had heard that many notable people considered the Colonies the hope of the human race, though I didn't pretend to understand their reasoning. At the moment, I couldn't remember very much of what we'd had in school about Mars, and I doubted that Ross could, either.

"Just because you and I wouldn't like it doesn't mean that everyone who goes is crazy," I ventured.

Ross wasn't to be budged. "What else can you call it?" he said angrily. "That's one thing I always liked about you; you weren't one of those spacestruck girls—girls who go around with their heads in the clouds thinking there's something worthwhile about wanting to get away from the problems we've got right here. You were interested in settling down."

"I'm still interested in settling down."

"Well, act like it, then."

"I don't know how we got started on this, Ross," I said. "I wouldn't be staying on Mars, anyway—"

"You aren't going at all!"

"Well, I said I wasn't."

He didn't even hear me. "Everything else aside, you can't afford to miss a year of college. Even if I'd let you be away that long."

"Dad thinks I could study on the ship."

"You've got to get your teaching credentials just as soon as you can, so you can work while I'm in law school."

"Oh? You mean you'd rather I didn't do anything that might interfere with my supporting us?" I was close to tears. I had planned to teach while Ross was in law school, but after all, that wasn't exactly why we were getting married.

"I mean I won't let you disrupt everything we've planned,

Melinda. I gave in about the summer vacation, but not about this. You can't go, and that's final."

You can't go. Not any discussion about what I might miss out on, or how hurt Dad would be if I refused. Just, *you can't.*

"Since when have you had the right to make my decisions?" I asked.

His hand closed tight on mine. "You're my girl, Mel. You've always been my girl."

And I always had been. It had never seemed like a restriction before. But suddenly I saw those safe, scheduled years stretching out ahead of us, with Ross always telling me how things were going to be; with no chance to be myself, Melinda Ashley, ever at all. And we weren't even married yet. Once we were married, would he object every time I tried to make up my own mind?

"Maybe so, but I'm not your property, Ross," I said slowly. "And if I want to go with Dad, I will."

Even then, if he had kissed me, I might not have gone through with it. I might have got back my normal composure and said, "It's lucky I *don't* want to," or some such thing. But he didn't. He punched the exit switch and rammed the steering wheel back into place, ready to take manual control of the car as it came off the expressway onto the next ramp.

"I'll take you out to your grandmother's, Mel," Ross said icily. "I can see you're too tired to talk sensibly. We'd better pick some other night to go into Portland."

I didn't object. I slid over to the far side of the seat and stared straight ahead, blinking back the tears, while the lights of the Expressway blurred and receded. *Oh Ross*, I was thinking, *what's happened to us? How can we be acting this way when we love each other?*

It was not until I was standing in the driveway at Gran's, with my luggage and school stuff piled beside me and the roar of the departing car drowning the familiar welcome of the surf, that I realized that I had committed myself. Somehow the argument had gotten turned around, and I had ended up defending the very thing I had wanted Ross's help in getting out of! I looked up through the trees and saw the stars, and for the first time it really hit me that I might be going out there. Into *space*. Even though I hated the idea.

I pushed the thought away. After all, I wasn't going to let it change anything! Quickly I turned toward the lighted house, and as I ran up the steps I felt warm and safe again because I knew that however far away I went, these solid redwood walls would be waiting for me.

Chapter 3

When I remember that week at Gran's, it's all soft colors: blues and grays and greens and, on bright days, a wash of yellow. Earth is like that, you know. On Mars colors are harsh, in spite of the weak sunlight; the orange sand contrasts sharply with the unvarying light pink sky. On Earth everything's muted by that lovely cushion of moist, thick air.

But at the time, I didn't know how I'd miss the gray days. It was typical Northwest weather—hours of clouds and drizzle usually do outnumber the hours of sunshine—yet often enough I accused it of having made a deliberate effort to match my mood.

On the first morning I skipped breakfast and walked several miles along the beach, stopping every so often to sit and watch the tide go out. The bay was calm and the widening swath of pebbles along the water's edge glistened wetly; overhead the gulls wheeled. It was all the same as the picture I'd been holding in my mind for so long. It didn't have its usual effect on me, though. The comfort of homecoming I'd felt the night before hadn't lasted, and Maple Beach seemed as unreal as everything else did—the thought of the trip, Dad's presence, the horrible lost sensation whenever I realized how things stood between me and Ross. I kept wondering, *When am I going to wake up?*

Part of the trouble, probably, was that Ross and I hadn't ever been really mad at each other before. I actually had never quarreled with a boy, a boy I cared about, that is. I suppose it doesn't sound very earthshaking; couples fight every day without any catastrophic results. I knew Ross would call me sooner or later. But our relationship had been so good, so smooth, and now, since it was spoiled, I didn't see how we could ever have the same kind of happiness again. I'd have given a lot to be back in school with graduation still ahead.

Naturally, I blamed the whole mess on Mars.

One part of me knew perfectly well that it was not Dad's fault, and that he had given me that ticket to Mars with the best of intentions. Knowing it didn't help. Another part of me was wishing very hard that I had never heard of Mars, and that Dad had stayed away a year longer, or maybe forever. Yet at the same time I wanted to be with him; I didn't want to give that up. It wasn't fair that I'd never had a chance to be with my parents! And he must care a lot about having me, to go to so much trouble. Suppose I refused to go; would he turn the job down? I'd hate that, but then, underneath I'd hate it if he didn't.

I really wanted to make Dad happy. I might have come to Mars on that account, even if Ross and I hadn't fought; I like to think I would. But I'll have to say that I might not have. To me, the prospect was in itself disturbing, aside from the question of the year I'd miss.

It's said that there are two kinds of people who don't like the idea of space travel: people with acrophobia—fear of heights, that is—and people with claustrophobia. I'm sure that's true, because in a spaceship a person's literally falling through millions of miles of emptiness, and at the same time tightly enclosed. But there's much more to it than that. I was never particularly bothered either of those ways; what troubled me more was just the thought of leaving Earth, even temporarily. It may be stating the obvious, and I may sound like somebody's grandmother, but for countless ages billions of people were born, lived, and died on Earth who would have been simply horrified at the mere mention of leaving. After all, it's only in recent years that anyone's had a choice, and the percentage of people who do leave is practically infinitesimal. A good deal's said about how the Colonies are booming, but the actual population of the Moon and Mars is still small; and in spite of all the publicity about its being the new fad in Cook's Tours, there aren't as many tourists as you might think. Lowering the fares might help, but somehow I don't think that the average citizen is terribly anxious to blast off. I don't believe that my feeling was too unusual.

Most of the kids who say they want to go into space have never come face-to-face with the opportunity. They haven't any real prospect of going, and inside they know it. Most of the ones who do go—homesteaders, scientists, TPC employees, astronauts, and so forth—are either so wrapped up in their careers that they wouldn't notice if the sun turned blue, or they've got a very mature orientation. There are exceptions; I knew one girl who wanted to be an astronaut so much that she spent her school years ignoring earthly pursuits entirely. (They didn't take her.) But by and large, a person needs an awfully adult outlook to be happy off our native planet.

I didn't have it. I still equated "human" with "Terrestrial." To me, "natural" meant "the way things are on Earth," and anything else was wrong, somehow. So when I considered going to Mars, I started to think about all the things on Earth that people normally take for granted—trees, grass, birds, oceans . . . the list is endless—and I knew that those things wouldn't be found anywhere else. Only I didn't know enough to imagine what would be found instead. Then I remembered how often I'd heard Martian cities, which are domed, compared to the underground portions of Terrestrial cities; and I hate underground cities! Canned air. Artificial lighting day and night. All in all, it just didn't sound like an ideal vacation spot.

Luckily, Dad wasn't around much during the week before our departure; he had some people to see. So he didn't realize that I worried for two whole days, hardly eating a thing. Gran thought I was moping over Ross, which of course was partly true. We didn't go to church on Sunday because Gran wasn't feeling up to it. She wasn't hungry at dinnertime, either, and didn't mind when I heated some soup for us and let it go at that.

Most days I spent a lot of time on the beach. It was too cold to swim and there wasn't any sun to lie in, but I went anyway. I sat on the wet rocks below the house and looked out toward the gray, misty horizon, thinking that however far it looked, that distance was just a drop in the bucket compared to the distance between Earth and Mars. Then I thought about the cookout Ross and I might be having if it were just an ordinary summer Sunday, how we'd lie beside the beach fire after dark, and listen to the waves pounding the rocks . . . and when I climbed the rickety old wooden stairs back to the garden, my face was as wet as my jacket and scarf were.

On Monday morning Dad took me into Portland to apply for my passport and Colonial entry visa. We went to the medical center first, and I submitted to a computer interview, followed by an all-too-thorough examination; then we had to wait while they ran the lab tests. I was glad that Gran had insisted that I eat a good breakfast, yet in a way I hoped that maybe they would find some little thing wrong. It would be such a simple way out of the whole business! But the report came out saying that I was extremely healthy, although about ten pounds underweight, and the receptionist laughed and said the spacelines weren't likely to turn me down for *that*. I knew that the results were okay, of course, when she handed me the printout without calling me back to discuss it with a doctor.

I did have to talk to the psychiatrist, Dr. Spencer, though. The psychiatric examinations they do for temporary visas are just a matter of form, nothing like what prospective colonists go through. Still, they wouldn't let any out-and-out psychotics on board a ship; too many people are cooped up too closely, for too long. Nor, for that matter, would the Colonies want to admit anyone potentially dangerous, even for a short time.

I had to sign a file-search permit and as I went in I could see the girl entering it into the computer, so I knew that the doctor had all my up-to-date school records in front of him and didn't need to ask me any questions at all. Still, we talked for a while, and he impressed me as a kind, friendly person, not at all like those cold, clinical interns that are sent out to school so often. I felt that I was wasting his time because we weren't saying anything significant: just what my hobbies were and what I planned to major in at college. Then, all of a sudden, he asked me what was making me so unhappy.

It caught me off guard; I hadn't thought it showed. Finally I stammered, "Well, I—I had a fight with my fiancé." Technically, Ross wasn't my fiancé yet, but it amounted to the same thing.

Dr. Spencer agreed that it was no wonder I was upset, and he didn't get at all nosy about the sort of relationship that Ross and I had. He seemed to feel that it was my own business. But he didn't let the subject drop there. Gently, he asked, "Do you really want to go to Mars, Melinda?"

Well, he was the first person who hadn't simply assumed either that I did or that I didn't, and maybe that's why I answered honestly. Of course, I knew that anything you tell a doctor is absolutely confidential and can't even be put in the data bank without your consent. I broke down and explained the whole thing, that I didn't want to go, and that I would give anything to be able to think of a way out of it.

A psychiatrist doesn't advise you; he just sits there and doesn't indicate whether he approves or disapproves of what you're saying, although if he's got a sympathetic personality like Dr. Spencer's, he manages to give you a feeling that even if it's something awful there's going to be a way to work things out. So I didn't expect to be handed a ready-made solution to all my problems. I guess I did sort of hint, though, that if he were to say that he didn't think the trip would be good for me . . . .

"Melinda," he told me, "I'll be frank with you. If I were interviewing you for an emigration permit, I wouldn't approve it. Emigration's too permanent; any colonist other than a child has got to be sure that she knows what she wants, that the way she feels about things isn't going to undergo any substantial change. It's necessary not only from her point of view but from the Colony's, because they can't afford any washouts. But in your case—"

I started to say that I was sure about the future I wanted, had always been sure, and that my chief trouble was with the whole plan being disrupted.

"That's where we disagree," Dr. Spencer said. "I don't think you're sure at all. You *want* to be sure, which is another thing entirely. Perfectly normal at your age, of course."

"Would I be any more sure if I went to Mars?" I asked.

"Quite possibly. You could surprise yourself. I'm not going to help you decide whether to go or not; that's up to you. But I have no grounds whatsoever for denying you a temporary visa. You're in fine shape emotionally." He smiled. "It's obvious that you aren't a danger either to yourself or to anyone else."

That was the first time I'd stopped to think that happiness and mental health aren't exactly the same. I was more miserable than ever before in my life, and he thought I was fine! Talking it out did help, however, even though it seemed rather odd that Dr.

Spencer couldn't see how sure I was about wanting to stay put at Maple Beach.

When we got home, I went upstairs to try to get my belongings into some kind of order. My duffel bags from school stood in the corner where I'd dropped them; so far I hadn't had the heart to open anything except my overnight case. But I knew I'd have to pack for the trip, or at least do something with the things that I wouldn't be taking. What should you take to Mars, anyway?

My ticket said "twenty kilos maximum"; and, Dad had explained, the maximum isn't just the free allowance, it's the total allowance. If you exceed it, you have to take something out before they'll let you board. Moreover, it includes the clothes you wear, your purse, and anything else you want to keep with you, for they weigh you along with your luggage and subtract your medical certificate weight. That seems like carrying things to extremes, but weight is critical on a spaceship, and I suppose if they didn't check closely people would bring on all they could carry, particularly the homesteaders.

But the weight limit wasn't too much of a concern to me because I actually didn't care much what I took. I put in some of my permanent fabric school clothes and the silky robe Dad had given me for Christmas, without having any idea of what would be appropriate. I came across two whole sets of washable lingerie Gran had bought for me once, and realized that at last they'd come in handy; I always wore disposable lingerie, but I'd heard that disposables aren't available in the Colonies. At the last moment, I stuck in my dear old hand-knit sweater, the one made of real sheep's wool. It was heavy, but so what? There wasn't that much else I'd be needing. I didn't give any thought to sportswear or date clothes at all, let alone the possibility that Colonial styles might be different.

As I finished putting things away, I looked wistfully around the room. I had always loved it, though it hadn't been really mine for the past six years. Gran had used it for a guest room while I was at school, but some of my things remained in the dresser drawers and on the top shelf of the closet.

Someday, when I inherit the house from Gran, I'll be told that the bedroom furniture is worth a great deal of money and that it would be wise to have it auctioned off. I won't agree, though, because it *belongs* in that room. It's all original, and hasn't ever been replaced as the living room set has. It was antique in style even in the twentieth century when the house was built; now it's antique in fact also. Gran offered to get me new furniture when I first came to her as a child, for she thought I might want something more appropriate for a little girl than a dark polished mahogany bedstead with ornate carved headboard and a heavy matching chest of drawers. But I wouldn't let her. So she settled for new blue-figured wallpaper with matching curtains, a white bedspread, and a fluffy white rug. That rug was still beautifully fluffy and white as I knelt there packing beside an open drawer. I hate bare, modernistic things.

After I was through I stood at the window and looked out across the grayed redwood deck at the sunlight glinting off the water through a brief break in the clouds. There was a ship near the horizon, moving slowly; I wondered where it was bound. Once people traveled on ships of the sea, not just for pleasure cruises but to get from one place to another. Once the word "ship" itself evoked pictures of wind and salt water, not of black emptiness and hard glittering stars. I wished that I had lived in those times.

On the bed I'd piled some odds and ends that seemed hardly worth keeping; I gathered them up and went across the hall to Gran's room to see if she wanted any of them.

Gran was sitting by the window with her feet on the ottoman. Her magazine was open but she wasn't reading; her eyes were closed. I hesitated in the doorway, realizing unhappily that I hadn't paid much attention to Gran since I'd been home, hadn't offered much in the way of sympathy for the illness that had kept her away from graduation. Just then she sat up and looked at me, and I went over and kissed her lightly on the cheek.

"Hello, Melinda dear," Gran said brightly. "How did it go this morning? Did they give you your visa?"

"Yes, with no trouble at all. I guess I convinced them that I'm of good character and not too likely to get sick way out in the middle of nowhere." I sat down on the edge of the ottoman. "Are you feeling better today, Gran?"

"Much better, thank you. Your father wants me to come to Florida to see you off. I might do just that; I could stay overnight and come back to Portland on Sunday, if it seemed too much of an effort to do the round trip in one day."

"That would be wonderful," I said, though I hadn't gotten to the stage of picturing the trip in detail. Florida, Canaveral Terminal—we'd be going there Saturday morning.

"Melinda," Gran said, "I haven't given you anything for graduation yet. I was waiting for a time when you weren't so preoccupied."

I flushed guiltily. Gran went on, "Get my jewel box, will you, dear?"

I went over to her dressing table and picked up the well-remembered green leather case that she'd shown me so often when I was a child. Gran took it from me. As she opened it, I caught sight of the locket that had been handed down from our ancestor, Melinda Stillwell, and I reached out to touch the gleaming gold.

"Do you remember how I used to play with this?" I asked.

"Very well. You used to love to hear about the covered wagon pioneers."

"I used to wish I could have been one of them. Everything was so simple then. Not all citified and scientific, like today."

She made no comment. Instead, she opened the bottom drawer of the case and took out a necklace of large silver beads. "These aren't of great value," she told me, "but they were your mother's. She treasured them, and perhaps you will, too, more than anything new I could buy you."

They were lovely. Dear Gran, she knew me so well! I'd always wanted something of Mother's to keep. My eyes filled as I clasped them around my neck and thanked her. For a moment I felt like throwing my arms around her, though Gran had never been one for hugging and kissing.

Putting the jewel box aside, I looked at her thoughtfully. "Gran," I asked, "did you know that my mother wanted to go to Mars?"

"Of course, dear. She wrote me all about it."

"Why didn't you ever tell me?"

"Why, when she died you were such a little girl; it wouldn't have meant anything to you then. Later—well, I never happened to mention it, that's all."

It seemed strange that she hadn't, considering how often she'd talked of my mother. I stared at the framed portrait on Gran's bedside table, the portrait of Mother when she was my age. "Why did she want to, do you think?"

Gran smiled. "Anne was always proud of our family's traditions."

"Dad said something like that. I don't see—"

"I might as well confess, dear, that I didn't want you to get too interested in the Colonies," Gran admitted. "I was afraid that if you heard your parents had once planned to emigrate, you'd want to pick right up where they left off, as soon as you were old enough."

"Oh, no!"

"I couldn't be sure. You're very like Anne in many ways, Melinda. Underneath."

I couldn't be too much like her, I thought, because I certainly didn't share her ambition. And I didn't understand what Dad and Gran had meant at all, referring to family traditions the way they had. *I* was the one who cared about history; I was the one who wanted to live in the house at Maple Beach forever, even if it wasn't modern.

"I was very selfish, I know that," Gran sighed. "You were all I had, dear. You still are."

Somehow I hadn't thought of that side of it. I began quickly, "Gran, if *you* don't want me to—"

She went right on. "However, your father's been hoping to see Mars for many years, and I know how happy Anne would be that he's got the chance. I know how happy she'd be, Melinda, to see you going with him in her place. So I can't be sorry. Especially since it's only a visit and you'll be coming back."

"Of course I'll be back, Gran darling," I promised. "Just you wait, before you know it I'll be back here again, here to stay."

Even then, I realized what a good thing it was that she hadn't let me finish what I'd begun to say. Because it wouldn't have been an honest out, though I did love her; I could never have looked Dad in the face, pretending to be making a big sacrifice for Gran's sake. With what she'd said about my going making Mother happy, though—well, I couldn't help wondering what Gran would have thought if Ross and I had presented a united front and I'd announced that I wasn't willing to do it. The whole thing was getting just too complex. Why did everything seem to be conspiring to get me on board that ship, when a few days before I'd have put a trip to Mars high on the list of totally pointless occupations?

After that talk with Gran, I more or less resigned myself to the inevitable. I did my best to respond to Dad's enthusiasm. I even phoned Julie and told her the news; she was tremendously excited and was all for giving me a going-away party. I had to make some excuse about not having time, though I'd have loved to see

Julie and Lorene again; I just couldn't have gone to a party without Ross. Anyway, a party would only have resulted in a lot of useless bon voyage gifts, none of which would have fit into my weight allowance.

But in spite of the fact that I was going ahead with the preparations, I don't think I really believed in them. All that week, in the back of my mind there was a glimmer of hope, the thought of the one thing that could bring an end to the whole senseless business. Suppose when Ross phoned to apologize—and of course, he *would* phone—we were to end up setting our wedding date? I knew the only way I could back out would be for Ross and me to go to Dad and say, "Sorry, but we're getting married right away."

Perhaps Ross knew it, too. Because he didn't phone at all. Every time the phone rang, that whole week, I rushed to it; never once was it for me.

So, one by one, the days slipped past, and long before I was ready it was Friday morning, then Friday afternoon, and finally, Friday evening. My last night on Earth, for the time being at any rate, and it seemed as if something dramatic ought to happen at such a time. Yet as it was, I didn't do anything very significant and spent most of the evening fooling around the house, fixing my hair, and sorting out stuff that there hadn't been room to pack. I went down to the beach for an hour or so, as usual. An awful waste! Or was it? On second thought I'm glad it was a "normal" evening, considering the wild things I've done since.

Chapter 4

Departure from Earth was a less shattering experience than I had expected. It's all made to seem very normal—too normal, perhaps. If I'd been looking forward to something exciting, like the sailing of an old-time ocean liner, I'd have been disappointed.

Saturday morning we flew to Florida, and that was just like any flight, of course. Gran didn't go with us after all. She didn't even see us off at the airport, so the last memory I have of her is as she stood on the deck of the house, waving, with it all falling away beneath us as the taxi copter lifted us out toward the Portland-bound traffic pattern. In no time at all the house was only a speck, hardly discernible against the dazzle of the sea. I twisted around in my seat and looked back as long as I could, wanting to slow the passing moments.

I didn't cry. The year ahead was just something to be got through, that's all. I was determined to endure it. I didn't feel any sense of loss, for I didn't know yet how things are changed by time.

It was raining when we left Portland, and it was raining in Orlando, too. We took another taxi copter from the airport out to

Canaveral Terminal. We could have waited for the scheduled helicopter; there was plenty of time. We had over three hours to make our connection, but we couldn't afford to take any chances because we were booked to go up on the last shuttle.

People who haven't known much about space often don't realize that the big interplanetary ships, the Colonial transports, never touch Earth. They're too big and unstreamlined; they aren't built for atmospheric flight. More than that, it would take far too much fuel to get off again. Then, too, there's the radioactivity from the nuclear drive, since the shielding of the passenger decks doesn't protect anything outside.

I'd learned all this in school, I guess, but it hadn't really penetrated, and at first I'd thought we'd be going directly onto the *Susan Constant*. Dad had explained it to me back at Gran's, though, so when we got to the terminal I knew more or less what to expect. In fact, I knew just enough so that I was beginning to feel not only unhappy, but nervous. Darn Ross anyway; why had he needed to say what he had about the perils of space travel?

Isn't it funny how you can accept one thing as a perfectly natural, inevitable risk of living, and be all upset over something else just because it's less common? I was well enough aware that there hadn't been an accident on a scheduled spaceship for years, and that in terms of percentages, a regular airliner was a lot more likely to crash. As a matter of fact, I knew that a car was a worse prospect than either, according to statistics; and I'd never thought twice about driving, any more than I'd questioned the flight from Portland to Orlando. Yet when I looked out across the field at those slim, gleaming rockets poised on their launch-pads, I got a definitely queasy feeling in my stomach.

You hear a lot about the discomforts of spaceships—acceleration, zero gravity, and all that—but you don't stop to think that most of it doesn't apply to commercial liners. The spacelines don't expect you to be astronaut material any more than the airlines expect passengers to have the physique of test pilots. They do accelerate at several gravities and the shuttles go into zero-g when the power's cut; even the big ships are weight-less for a short time while they maneuver, before they put on spin. That's one reason a medical exam is required for your pass-port. But it's not anything like what astronauts go through. And besides, what with the spacesickness shots you get, and the tranquilizers—well, it just doesn't bother you.

But beforehand, your idea of all this is rather hazy. At least mine was. I looked around the terminal at the people getting ready to leave—middle-aged, many of them, and families with small children, babies, even—and told myself that there couldn't be anything to get panicky about. But it didn't change the way I felt inside.

Of course, only a small percentage of these people were going to Mars. Most of them were on their way to Luna City and the majority would be away only a few weeks for a business trip or a short vacation. There's lots of traffic between Earth and the Moon all the time; departures for Mars are comparatively rare. If we missed the *Susan Constant* there wouldn't be another for months. I confess that I'd have been awfully glad if I could have figured out some way to miss it.

That's not entirely true, though. When I looked at Dad and saw how elated he was, I knew I wouldn't want anything to spoil his trip, no matter how I felt secretly.

The one thing I just couldn't understand was why he was so anxious to go. I admit that most of the past week I'd avoided mentioning Mars, and usually when he had started to talk about the trip, I'd managed to change the subject. So maybe it was my own fault. I don't think Dad knew how to explain it, though. This longing to see Mars had been in the background of his mind for so long, it seemed perfectly natural to him, the way my wanting to stay at Maple Beach seemed natural to me.

"It won't be long now, Mel!" he said, as we carried our baggage over to the long TPC desk under the revolving triple globes emblem.

"I guess not," I agreed.

He grinned at me. "I suppose you think I'm behaving just like a little boy."

I said, "Of course not, Dad," though that was exactly what I thought.

"I'm as excited as a little boy," he told me. "I'm more thrilled than I used to be at Christmas. I remember the Christmas I was eight, my dad gave me a model ship—the *Fortune*, it was, which had just been put into service at the time. I feel like acting the way I did then! However, I'll try to maintain the appropriate dignity."

"Is an executive supposed to be dignified?" I inquired, laughing.

"Well, I'm representing the firm, after all; can't give anyone the impression I'm an overgrown kid playing spaceman." Suddenly he sobered, and put his hand on my arm. "Mel, honey—if only your mother were here. She wanted this so much."

I touched Mother's silver beads, which filled the neckline of my suit. "Dad," I asked, "what did Mother's family traditions have to do with her wanting to go to Mars?"

He turned to me, surprised. "Why, they were pioneers, that's all. One of them was on the original *Mayflower*, I think; anyway they went west step by step, until finally they got to Oregon."

"I don't see the connection. They weren't doing it for the good of science, or anything like that. They just wanted—"

I was interrupted by the loudspeakers. *"Paging Melinda Ashley,"* they blared. *"Melinda Ashley, please come to the passenger service desk."*

"Excuse me, Dad." I pushed through to the other side of the line and crossed over to the center of the rotunda, where I could see the Passenger Service sign. "Phone call for you, Ms. Ashley," the girl said, motioning me over to one of the phone booths that ringed the desk. I punched in the code she gave me and the viewplate lit up. It was Ross.

I was so relieved to see him that for a moment I couldn't speak. I'd given up hope, had been convinced that I wasn't going to hear from him before I left, and now he'd called after all. At the very last minute—how like Ross!

"So you really meant it, Mel," Ross said. "I didn't believe it, till your grandmother told me where to reach you. I was going to ask you to go to Portland tonight for that dinner we missed."

I wondered if that was true, and then suddenly knew it was.

Ross expected me to be there, waiting, whenever he decided to make plans. It had never occurred to him that I wouldn't be; I always had been before. He'd stopped being mad and was ready to forget the whole topic of Mars, and he was assuming that went for both of us.

"I did mean it, Ross," I said. "We lift off a little while from now."

"So I see." He looked rather helpless and confused, as if he hardly believed that I could defy him. Ross wasn't used to that.

"Please try to understand," I pleaded. "I promised Dad. He can't help it that this trip will last longer than the summer."

"Can't he? He must really want you, all right, I'll say that. It takes pull to get a place on one of those ships on short notice. My father had to fix it up for somebody once. He says space is normally booked years in advance."

"Dad's firm had a standing reservation. If they'd chosen some other man his wife would have gone."

"They sure wouldn't have had any trouble unloading the extra ticket at a big profit." Suddenly Ross brightened. "Well, I suppose you're right, Mel. I've been pretty unreasonable. If your dad insists that you go with him, naturally you've got to. You don't want to get him down on you. After all, he's putting you through college."

"Ross, surely you don't think that's why I—"

"I still call it a crazy waste of time. But you're doing the sensible thing; we'll just have to make the best of it, and pick up where we left off when you get back."

"But it isn't like that at all!" Covering my hand with my purse,

I reached over and shut off the video because I didn't want Ross to see the tears that were stinging my eyes.

"Mel? Hey, something's the matter with this phone connection. The picture's gone."

"Is it?"

"Yes. I can't see you, but the audio's coming through. Give me the extension, Mel, and I'll redial."

"There isn't time," I lied. "They're calling my flight."

"So soon? Well, good-bye, Mel. I'll write."

"Write? To *Mars?*" For some reason that struck me as funny and I started to laugh, though because I was crying it came out as more of a choke.

"Well, radio—whatever it is that people do. Look, Mel, you're still my girl. Remember that you're my girl, and you're going to marry me."

"I'll remember," I whispered. "Good-bye, Ross."

I wiped my eyes and started back across the rotunda. I should be happy, I thought. Ross wasn't thinking of breaking up. Nothing had changed between us; the trip wasn't going to make any difference. It was as if the fight had never happened.

Only it still seemed all wrong. Maybe it was just the way he had of wording things. The way he said *you're my girl*, not *I love you.* Would I have noticed that before we quarreled? I was going to marry Ross, but on the phone he hadn't once said that he loved me! When you love someone you should say so, shouldn't you?

But I hadn't said so, either.

"What was that all about?" Dad asked, as I joined him.

"Just a school friend," I told him. "Saying good-bye."

"How about some lunch?" he suggested. It wasn't time to re-port to the gate yet, and we wouldn't be able to leave the board-ing lounge once they'd stamped our passports.

"I'm not very hungry."

"It will do you good."

"Will it? Won't I get spacesick?"

"That's what they give shots for. Come on, we've got time to kill now."

"You're as bad as Gran!" I said, but I followed him toward the restaurant.

I've sometimes wondered if the trip would have been different for me if I hadn't had lunch at the Interplanetary Terminal that day. How can you plan, when the most trivial decision might change the course of things?

The restaurant was jammed when we went in and there was a long waiting line at the buffet. By the time we'd selected our food we had only half an hour left, and we found ourselves stuck with loaded trays, without an empty table anywhere in sight.

"We'll have to share," Dad said. "Look, there's a couple of seats."

The table he pointed to was occupied by a young man, alone, who seemed totally absorbed in the book he was reading while he ate. I started to protest that I'd hate to intrude, but Dad had al-ready spoken. "Pardon me, would you mind if we sat here?"

The man looked up and answered cordially, "No, of course not, sir. Sit down." He moved a small bag from the chair beside him and shifted his empty tray onto the floor. We piled ours on top of it after arranging our dishes on the table.

"We're in a hurry; they'll be calling our flight soon," I apologized.

"The shuttle for the *Susie?* I'm on it, too." The young man stared at me as if there were something astonishing in the fact that we happened to have the same destination. Then he smiled. "Did you ever try to do two things when there was only time for one? I've been having to choose between this book, which isn't in my weight allowance, and this steak, which is probably the last one I'll ever eat."

At this, I was the one to stare. "The last steak you'll ever eat? Don't you like it?"

"Sure, but I'm on my way back to the Colonies."

"Don't they have steak in the Colonies?"

Startled, he put his fork down again. "We couldn't raise cattle on Mars. They couldn't breathe the atmosphere any more than people could, and growing food for them would mean cutting down on more important crops."

"Oh, I didn't think about that." I blushed. The idea of a domed, pressurized cattle range was pretty ridiculous, I realized. "Please don't let us interrupt you," I said. "Go ahead and finish."

I nibbled at my own lunch but as he ate, I watched him. He was a few years older than I was, probably in his early twenties, with wavy brown hair, cut rather short, and gray eyes. And there was something about the way he moved that puzzled me. Very slow and deliberate, as if he were thinking about it.

"All passengers for the 13:45 shuttle, connecting with the S.S. Susan Constant, *check in please,"* announced the loudspeakers. *"All passengers for the S.S.* Susan Constant, *bound for Mars, report to gate three to weigh in."*

"That's us, I'm afraid," Dad said, taking a final bite of his sandwich.

The young man closed his book and laid it down. "Might as well leave it for the busboy," he said regretfully. "It's a good thriller, but I doubt if it'll find its way into New Terra's electronic library. I'll never know how it came out."

"It can't weigh much," I protested. "Take it along. Surely they'll let you keep it."

"Not a chance. They never make any exceptions; a fellow I know lost a good phone cam by miscalculating."

"Couldn't he have mailed it?"

"He could if he'd had that kind of money—more than the thing was worth, by a lot."

I don't know why I said what I did then. I didn't even know his name, and I've never been quick to take up with people. There was just something about him, I guess, that made me want to talk to him again.

"Let me carry your book aboard," I offered, to my own surprise. "My duffel bag was nearly half a kilo under what I expected, so I must be entitled to be that much heavier than before at the gate."

"Would you? Say, that's awfully nice of you." He handed it over. "You can read it, too, when the trip begins to get monotonous."

"I'd like to," I agreed, though at the moment monotony was the least of my worries.

"All passengers for the 13:45 shuttle..." the public address system began again. We gathered up our things and started for the gate. There was another long line ahead of us at the entrance to the boarding lounge. All the passengers who had friends or relatives seeing them off had waited till the last minute to say good-bye, naturally, so there were a lot more people crowded around than could possibly fit into one shuttle. Couples were hugging and kissing each other, babies were yelling, and old ladies were crying; it was hectic. It was a relief to have our passports checked and our weights recorded, and get through into the red-carpeted lounge.

I wasn't overweight at all, even with the book, probably because I'd eaten so little the past few days. They were particular, though. The woman ahead of me had a long argument with the flight attendant over her little boy's fleece-lined jacket. "But it's cold on Mars," she kept insisting.

"Not where you'll be going, ma'am. And it puts him over his allowance, so I'm afraid we can't let him wear it unless you want to give up something else. That's your privilege, of course."

"People are funny," our friend said to me softly. "Imagine starting out for Mars without knowing that a coat's just about the most useless article anybody could cart along."

"I thought Mars really was cold," I said, thinking of the treasured sweater that was taking up so much space in my own baggage.

"Well it is, outside—usually so cold that a coat couldn't be much help. But the groundcars are heated, and you can't get out of them without a pressure suit anyway, if you want to breathe." His tone was one of quiet amusement.

I felt my face grow hot, and I wished that I had taken the trouble to find out just a little more about where I was going beforehand. For the second time I'd displayed my ignorance. *Imagine starting out for Mars without knowing,* he'd said. How much else was there that he'd think me silly not to know?

The outer gate of the lounge was already open when we got there, and the elevators were taking people down to the access tunnel. Dad and I stepped into one just as the doors closed, and were separated from our lunch companion. There were several questions I had wanted to ask—for one thing, he'd said he was going *back* to the Colonies, so he must have been to Mars before; and for another, from the way he'd talked it was obvious that he was planning to stay. He didn't look like a person who'd want to live on Mars. But, I remembered, Dad and Mother had once wanted to live there, so I supposed you couldn't go by looks. Still, Dad had admitted that he felt like a little boy when it came to space, and there was definitely nothing little-boyish about this man. He had a kind of poise I hadn't felt in anyone before. I could tell he wasn't nervous about the trip, or excited, either. Happy, maybe, but not excited.

The access tunnel was deep below the field in order to withstand the rockets' blast force. As we came out of the elevator we saw that there was a monorail waiting for us. We were practically the last load to come down; the loudspeakers were warning,

"Last call for the 13:45 shuttle . . . all passengers for the S.S. Susan Constant *should now be checked in."*

In the tunnel my hands turned to ice. I sat there staring at the blue lights flashing past us, and I forgot all about the puzzling young man. All too soon we were whisked into another elevator, and up beside the ship. "We're in compartment B," Dad said casually. I wasn't ready to feel casual about being anywhere inside a spaceship.

The compartment had large, foam-padded seats, arranged in a circle, which converted to acceleration couches, reclining all the way back. The flight attendant was going around helping people to get all the straps fastened and seeing that everything was locked into place. Before long a second flight attendant came up through the center hatch from the lower compartment and began to dispense the spacesickness and tranquilizer shots. The people across from us had children, one of whom promptly set up a wail. I watched sympathetically. There are advantages to being four years old; you don't have to hide your feelings.

The flight attendant was very reassuring. "This won't hurt one bit, honey," she told the child. (It didn't; the stuff came in its own little tube, with a charge of compressed air or something—no needle.) The intercom speaker over our heads came to life with an amplified hum. "This is your captain speaking," a calm voice told us. "On behalf of Tri Planets Corporation I would like to welcome you aboard. Our flight time today will be four hours, fifteen minutes; rendezvous with the S.S. *Susan Constant* will be completed at approximately 23:00 Greenwich mean time. We are now in the final phase of countdown and will be lifting off about twenty minutes from now. If you have any questions, one of your flight attendants will be glad to help you." As he finished, soft music filled the compartment.

I lay back and fixed my eyes on the rivets in the ceiling, wondering if they would broadcast the countdown. On a plane you can at least see what's happening; they retract the boarding tube, taxi out to the runway, and so forth. In this ship there was nothing to watch. Any minute, I could be pinned to the couch by goodness knows how many g's of acceleration.

The seat next to me was empty. "It was reserved," the flight attendant said, "but the lady must have changed her mind at the last moment."

"She may show up yet," Dad said.

"It's too late now; we've sealed the airlock."

"Sealed" had a very permanent sound. I was thinking that the holder of that seat had shown a good deal of sense, when the young man whose lunch table we had shared appeared at the hatch. He came directly toward us and sat down beside me. "Hi," he said. "I heard there was an empty seat up here, and since you weren't in the compartment below—"

"Would you like your book?" I asked him. "My things are fastened down under here, but I guess there's time for me to get it. They won't weigh us any more, will they?"

"No, but don't bother now," he said. He reddened, for a moment losing the air of cool confidence. "Say, I hope you don't think that's why I came up!"

I shook my head, not knowing what to say.

He went on, smiling, "I wanted to know more about you, that's all. Are you a university student? Biology? Geology?"

"Not yet. Not on Mars, I won't be."

"Then how did they happen to let you emigrate? You're at least sixteen, so you can't be with homesteading parents—"

"I'm not an *emigrant*," I told him hastily. "Dad and I are on a trip. For his firm."

His eyes questioned the way in which I'd emphasized *"emigrant"* as if it were a category in which I'd hate to be placed. But then they lit up again. "I was sure you were something special," he said. "That is, I didn't think you could have the experience for a nonresident job on Mars; the career people we get are older."

"We?"

"The Colonies. I'm a Colonial citizen; I was born on Mars. My home's in the city of New Terra. By the way, I'm Alex Preston."

"And I'm Melinda Ashley." I was staring at him again. I simply couldn't think of Alex as a Martian! He wasn't any different from anyone else. Well, hardly any different; there were those few little things I'd noticed, but there wasn't anything Martian about those differences. Not that I could have said just what I thought Colonials would be like.

The music stopped and the intercom burst out again, evidently a recording this time. *"We are now beginning the final two minutes of countdown. Liftoff minus one hundred twenty seconds . . . one hundred second . . ."*

Alex buckled his straps with quick, practiced fingers and got his seat reclined just as the flight attendant hurried over for a last check before taking her own position. I glanced at Dad; his eyes were closed and there was a big smile on his face.

"*Eighty seconds . . . sixty . . . fifty . . .*"

Alex leaned over and touched my hand. "Why so quiet, Melinda? You're too solemn!"

"*Forty . . . thirty . . .*"

"Oh, I was just wondering what on earth I'm doing aboard this spaceship," I said. My voice sounded terribly tragic, I think.

He laughed. Then suddenly I did too, at the utter inappropriateness of the idiom, and when liftoff hit us we were both still laughing.

That was the second time I surprised myself with Alex. There were lots more times to come.

Part Two
SPACE

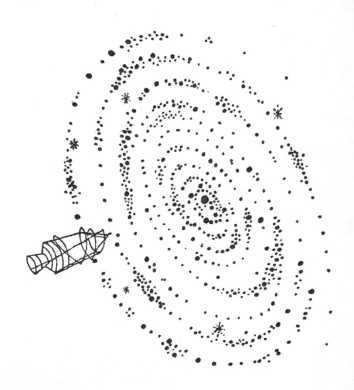

Chapter 5

Right from the beginning Alex was a person that I could talk to. I've never been a talkative person; that's one reason I'm shy and find it hard to make friends. I never know what to say to people. Even Dad and I never had a great deal to say to each other, which was too bad considering how much we both wanted to be close. But with Alex it was different. He always came out with something that I just naturally replied to, or at any rate something interesting enough to make me content with listening. Alex and I had more real conversations during the trip to Mars alone than Ross and I had had during the whole time we were dating. It seemed funny, because I was in love with Ross, while Alex was just someone I met boarding a ship.

The acceleration that accompanied liftoff wasn't really very bad (though I wouldn't want to go through it too often). I felt somewhat woozy and relaxed from the shots, but I don't think I would have panicked anyway. The worst part was the immobile, helpless feeling more than the actual pressure: the feeling of being unable to stir, to draw a deep breath, even. And the awful, ear-shattering noise! But those things didn't last long. Besides, there was Alex next to me, and I couldn't help but find comfort in the thought that he'd been through this before. Why that seemed more significant than the simple fact that shiploads of people did it every day, I couldn't imagine.

When the rockets cut off we went right into zero gravity, and it felt as if the bottom had dropped out of everything—which was exactly what had happened because there wasn't any "bottom" or "top" anymore. Zero-g has sometimes been called "free fall" and that's literally true, for it doesn't make any difference that the fall's not toward Earth, but away from it. This condition affects human beings in various ways. Some people love it; it's the kind of floating that used to be possible only in dreams. Others are just plain sick, and this would include a pretty large group if it weren't for those antinausea shots. Still others are terrified— after all, as I learned in Psychology I, fear of falling's one of the two basic fears a baby's born with—and I suspect that I would have come out in the latter category, except that Alex didn't let me.

He raised his seat, then started to undo his straps so that he could reach over and raise mine. The flight attendant rushed right over and started to protest. (She floated through the hatch upside down, as it happened—no wonder their uniforms have pants instead of skirts—and turned so that her feet pointed toward the "floor" more for the passengers' benefit than for any practical reason.) "Sir, passengers are not allowed to—"

Alex pulled his card wallet out of his pocket. "Even with this?" he inquired, holding something out to her.

"Sorry, Mr. Preston. Certainly you may unstrap."

I looked at him and asked, tactlessly maybe, "Are you a VIP or something?"

He smiled. "Not at all. It's just that I have a card to show that I know how to handle myself in zero-g." He released the lock on my seat and it sprang forward so that I was sitting up. "It used to be that they wouldn't let anyone unstrap on these short hauls, but as the proportion of experienced space travelers grew, so did the protests. Now they honor the cards. I'm afraid that won't help you or your dad, though."

"I don't want to move around!" I declared fervently.

"I won't argue because they aren't going to let you anyway. But you'd be surprised at how much fun it is once you get a taste of it."

"Where did you learn?" I asked. "You're not an astronaut, are you?"

"No. I learned on a trip to Phobos, when I was twelve. All Colonial kids do."

"For fun?"

"Partly. You might call it a compensation for the centrifuge, which isn't so pleasant."

"Centrifuge, like the way they test astronauts? Why did you have to do that if you weren't going to be one?"

"Because I knew that I might want to come to Earth someday. And Earth's gravity is three times what I was born to." He grinned at me. "If I hadn't trained for it, Earth to me would have been something like that liftoff was to you."

Slowly I took this in. I'd known Martian gravity was low, but the implications hadn't struck me before. No wonder he'd moved slowly and deliberately back at the terminal. "How could you train for it?" I asked.

"In a special gym, under spin. Ever since eighth grade, an hour a day. You work up gradually, of course. It prepares you to accept terrestrial gravity, but not to enjoy it. This is the first time I've been really comfortable since I landed last year!"

"I'm glad I wasn't born on Mars."

"That's one way of looking at it," he agreed. "But if you had been, you wouldn't have had to come to Earth; lots of people don't. It used to be that most families wanted their kids to go sooner or later, the way the early American colonists sent their sons home to England to be educated. But that attitude's getting to be old-fashioned."

"You're not sorry you came, are you?"

"No, I wouldn't have missed it for anything. I could have gotten my master's degree just as well on Mars, I suppose. But I wouldn't have seen as much."

"I should think," I said hesitantly, "that now you've had a chance to live normally—well, that it would be awfully hard for you to go back, if it weren't for the gravity, that is. I mean, it might be better for you if you hadn't come."

Alex stiffened. "What do you mean?"

"Well, you wouldn't have known what you were missing. That is, you'd have known, but you probably wouldn't have cared in the same way." I was struggling with what was, for me, an unfamiliar concept. It was hard to imagine anybody regretting having come to Earth; yet for someone who'd been born a

Martian, it must be terribly upsetting to come knowing that he couldn't stay long.

But Alex didn't understand me. "Perhaps I've given a wrong impression," he said quietly. "Melinda, I was kidding about not getting used to Earth gravity! I could have, of course, if I'd had any reason for wanting to stay."

I was confused, and sorry that I'd allowed the conversation to get so personal. It was none of my business why he was going back to Mars; perhaps his family needed him, or maybe he had run out of money and couldn't get a job. He wasn't a citizen of any country on Earth, after all.

He went on, "You're assuming quite a lot, aren't you, thinking that I'd be happier on Mars if I hadn't seen Earth?" There was a sharp tone in his voice; without meaning to, I'd somehow made him angry.

By that time all I wanted to do was drop the subject, but I asked, "What am I assuming?"

We were interrupted by the flight attendant who, much to my relief, had come to serve tea. The spacelines operate on the same theory as the airlines used to, which is that passengers will cause less trouble, and will think that they're getting more for their money, if they are kept constantly occupied with something to eat. Or maybe they feel that if anyone's nervous, the sight of other people eating will seem reassuring; and that's probably true. At any rate, in spite of its being just after lunch by Florida time and the middle of the night by Greenwich, we were offered a bountiful selection of such goodies as could be adapted to zero-g conditions, as well as our choice of coffee, tea, or soft drinks. The beverages came in closed containers with sipping tubes, for you can't pour a liquid that's weightless; you've got to suck.

Since most of us had to stay strapped down, we couldn't look at the view, and there were no viewports anyway. There was, however, a wide screen closed-circuit TV setup over our heads, on which they showed Earth. It was beautiful, but it was hard to take in the fact that it wasn't just a video, like so many I'd seen before. For this reason it didn't make a very deep impression on me until later when I saw the real thing from the *Susie.* Then, too, my mind was well occupied with the mere thought of being in space, plus the nagging question, *What was I assuming that he could have resented?*

Dad was deep in a discussion with the man on his left, who was a nonresident engineer returning to Mars from his biennial vacation. They'd found they had a lot to talk about, most of it hopelessly technical. So after we finished eating I was thrown back on Alex, although really I wished that I didn't have to be. I thought of pretending to be asleep, but I suspected that already he knew me too well to think I'd sleep under such conditions. He'd respect my privacy if I tried it, but his feelings might be hurt, and I didn't want that.

As it turned out, though, I had nothing to worry about. Our conversation was simply friendly, and I didn't once get the vague sense of inadequacy—that uncomfortable, unsure feeling—that Alex's response to my assumptions had brought on before.

Alex told me that he had come to Earth for a year of graduate work, and that he had just received his master's degree in business administration from the University of California. The Colonies, I learned, had a greater shortage of administrators than of scientists. He talked quite a bit about Mars, and it wasn't until afterward that I recognized any pattern in the way he described it.

"My folks were among the original settlers," he explained. "My dad works for TPC, which is why I could afford the trip to Earth; they discount fares for employees' families on top of the student rate. I'm taking a job with them myself for the time being, though someday I want to start a business of my own."

I wondered what sort of business, and why he thought that Mars would be a good place for it, but I didn't like to ask him. Alex went on, "Mom's a medical technician at St. John's Center."

"Have you any other relatives on Mars?"

"I've a sister, Alicia, who's thirteen. Then there's my cousin Paul and his family. Paul is a minister."

I don't know why that surprised me. Naturally there are churches in the Colonies just like anywhere else, but somehow you don't think of a minister as being interested in going to Mars. I found out that Paul had been born in New Terra, the same as Alex, and that his father had been one of the chaplains for the first little group of colonists and had helped to lay out the city.

"Paul's wife Kathy teaches in the West Dome elementary school," Alex said. "She and Paul already have three kids, and they're planning on five."

"*Five* children?"

"Yes, that's one of the advantages that draws homesteaders,

you know—no population tax like Earth's. In the Colonies it's the other way around; Mars wants more people, so couples who want large families can have them."

"What are some of the other advantages?" I inquired. I wasn't just making conversation, because I really wanted to know; it didn't seem as if there could be very many.

From the way Alex went on, however, Mars might as well have been the Promised Land. He mentioned a whole list of things, and what it boiled down to was Opportunity: not only the homesteaders' rights sort of opportunity, but the opportunity to build something, which maybe you don't find too often on Earth anymore. I didn't have any real conception then of what he was trying to say; I remember, though, how happy he looked when he spoke of it.

Alex also told me a lot about the *Susan Constant*, which he'd traveled in before. "The *Susie*'s not luxurious," he admitted. "A trip in her's not much like what I've heard of ocean cruises. She's an old ship, after all; she carried the first load of colonists, which is why we Martians have a special affection for her. On the whole she's comfortable enough. Some things will take getting used to, for you. Like water rationing."

I realized just in time that he must have grown up with water rationing and avoided stumbling into a remark that would make me feel foolish again. "Who was she named after?" I asked. "The *Susan Constant*, I mean."

"Not a 'who'—a ship from ancient history. One of the ones that founded the first permanent Virginia colony, in 1607."

"Did you study much history?"

"Quite a bit. Mostly on the side; I didn't have much time in college with my course load in business management, but I wanted to take advantage of the university library on Earth while I had it."

"I'm going to major in history," I told him.

"Then we have an interest in common." He sounded really glad about it, not just polite. "Did you ever stop to think what a coincidence it was, the first Elizabethan Age being the time of the first attempt to colonize North America, and the second Elizabethan Age being when the first offworld base was established on the Moon?"

I hadn't, in spite of Dad's folks being English and my having had world history in school as well as American history. But I knew about the starting of the Virginia colonies: the lost one, on Roanoke Island, and the one that succeeded, which became Jamestown. "That must have been an exciting age to live in," I said.

"Yes," he agreed. "But no more so than the early twenty-first century, do you think?"

"Well, more romantic, anyway."

"Really?" He paused, then went on, "There's a poem I like, about the colonization of America, *Western Star*, by Stephen Vincent Benét. Have you ever read it?"

"I don't think so. Do you know it by heart?"

"Well, not all of it; it's a whole book. I guess I remember one piece that particularly impressed me, though. One that refers to that same Virginia colony."

"Go ahead," I urged.

"I'll try." He thought for a moment, then began slowly, re-calling each line. If there were gaps, they weren't noticeable.

Is there Cathay beyond? Can Englishmen
Live there and plant there and breed there?
No one knows.
And yet, I know this much. It must be tried.
My one man's life hath seen this England grow
Into a giant from a stripling boy
Who fenced about him with a wooden sword
And prattled of his grandsire's wars. . . .
—The long, ruinous wars that sucked us dry,
. . . Nightmare, endless wars. . . .
Then we turned seaward. Then the trumpets blew.
And, suddenly, after the bloodshot night And the gropings in
the dark,
There were new men, new ships, and a new world.

There was another brief pause, and I was about to speak; but Alex remembered more and went on.

And yet, how did we dare, how did we dare! . . .
How did we dare to send our sailors out
Beyond all maps? . . .
I should know well, having some part in it,
And I look backwards on it, and I see
A grave young madman in a sober dress
Who, each day, plans impossibilities

And, every evening, sees without surprise
The punctual, fresh miracle come true.
And such were all of us. . . .

"That says it beautifully," I said. "How people of those times must have felt."

"Of course. But can you guess what really strikes me about it?"

"Besides what I just said?"

"Yes. It's about more than just the founding of Virginia. If you think of 'Cathay' in a symbolic sense, you only have to change three words in that excerpt to make it apply equally well to the exploration of space."

"What three words?"

"You just substitute 'Earthmen' for 'Englishmen,' 'Earth' for 'England,' and 'spaceward' for 'seaward.' "

I thought about it. "Why, that's true! Only make it 'Terra' instead of 'Earth,' so as not to spoil the meter." (It does work; he wrote it out for me later. I still have it in the folder where I keep hard copy.)

Alex smiled at me. "You'll do well in literature, besides in history."

Shyly, I smiled back. I tried to imagine Ross quoting poetry, and I couldn't. Not that Ross wouldn't be capable of remembering it; he had a memory like a computer for anything to do with finance or politics. He wasn't a bit like the men who can't talk on any topic except sports. But he never stopped to consider what would be likely to interest *me*. It was nice to be asked to share, for a change.

Astonishingly soon, the flight attendant was asking Alex to strap down again for rendezvous. We didn't have to recline this time since the maneuvering acceleration didn't exceed one gravity. (It felt like more, after weightlessness, but Alex assured me that it wasn't.) Then in a few moments we were back to zero-g again, and eventually some bumps indicated that we were docking with the *Susie*.

The lower compartment was nearest the exit, so we had to wait until it was emptied before they even let us unstrap. Then the flight attendant took us over to the hatch one at a time because she didn't want us crashing into each other. Climbing down the steps was easy enough, as long as we held on, and the other flight attendant was waiting at the bottom to help us through the double airlocks into the *Susan Constant*'s vestibule.

I was disappointed not to get even a glimpse of the *Susie* from the outside, but we never were outside; outside was vacuum. I had seen pictures and knew that she was huge, and shaped rather like a dumbbell, with the power plant in one sphere and the passenger decks in the other. But all I saw when I went aboard was a perfectly ordinary passageway with doors opening off at the sides and some steps going off at unbelievable angles. The *Susie*'s flight attendants, who wore red uniforms instead of blue, came to meet us and escort us to our staterooms. We wouldn't be allowed to walk around by ourselves until the ship broke contact with the shuttle and got her spin back.

That was where I was separated from Alex and also from Dad. I already knew that I'd be sharing my stateroom, for there's no room to spare on a spaceship and all the cabins are double. I wasn't prepared for just how small it would be, though. (If you've ever seen one of those "sleeping cars" they have in railroad museums, you've got the general idea.) There was barely room to stand up next to the double-deck bunk. And of course, no window. When the flight attendant closed the door behind him, I thought for a minute I was going to get claustrophobia after all, especially since that door wouldn't open again. Then I saw the sign on it: THIS EXIT IS AUTOMATICALLY SEALED DURING MANEUVERS AND ZERO-GRAVITY. IN CASE OF EMERGENCY RING FOR THE ATTENDANT. I spotted the bright red "panic button" and felt a little better.

The cabin lights were dim, and my roommate was lying on the lower bunk with a blanket pulled up over her and the safety net loosely fastened; all I could see of her was the back of a blonde head with short, tousled curls. She didn't move when I came in, or even when there was a knock and another flight attendant appeared with my duffel bag. I wondered if she was sick until I remembered that by ship's time it was nearly midnight.

I didn't want to go to sleep. I wanted to go out and find Dad. I wanted him to hug me tight and call me "Mel, honey" in that comfortable, affectionate way of his that I was coming to depend on, and maybe tell me once again just why it was that we were in this cramped, chilly cocoon of a ship on our way to Mars. But there was no way to do that, so without bothering to undress I clambered onto the upper bunk—which wasn't really *up*, of course—and buried my face in my arms.

Eventually I did fall asleep because I was worn out. Sometime later, about the time that would have been dawn if there were any dawn in space, we sailed. I never knew it. It was a low-g maneuver; I didn't wake to feel the weight seeping back into me as the *Susan Constant* slowly eased into her outbound orbit, toward another world.

Chapter 6

Dear old *Susie*—she was a good ship. It wasn't her fault that my
ten weeks aboard were for the most part such miserable ones.
Maybe if I hadn't drawn Janet Crane for a cabinmate, I would have
been spared a lot of trouble. Looking back, though, it's hard to
know how many of my problems were caused by her influence,
and how many I would have brought upon myself in any case.

It wasn't that Janet and I didn't get along. On the contrary, we
got along very well indeed, and decided right off that we saw eye
to eye about a lot of things. To start with, we must have been the
only two people on the ship who hated the very idea of going to
Mars. If they'd matched roommates by computer they couldn't
have done a better job of putting women with the same attitudes together.

Not that on the surface we were anything like each other.
Janet was much older, in the first place; eventually I found out
that she was almost thirty, though she didn't look it. More to the
point, she had striking silver-blonde hair, blue eyes, and a figure
that made me look very much the schoolgirl by comparison. And
her clothes! How she ever got a wardrobe like that into twenty
kilos, I'll never know. I suppose everything was featherweight. Of

course, she hadn't committed the faux pas of cramming in a sweater, not because she knew enough about Mars to foresee that she wouldn't need one, but because Janet wasn't the kind who wore sweaters.

But to give the idea that Janet Crane was more interested in her appearance than in anything else would be entirely wrong. She couldn't have cared less about the impression she made on men, or women either, except from the professional standpoint. Janet was a Scientist, with a capital "S"; she was a biologist, and someday she intended to be a top biologist.

The difficulty was that top biologists have to have experience with extraterrestrial microorganisms as well as with the life found on Earth. Most of them do a year of graduate work at the University of Mars before even getting their doctorates. Janet, who already had hers, had put the trip off because she didn't want to go; but the time had come when she couldn't advance any further in her career until she got it over with. Moreover, she wouldn't be eligible for the student fare much longer.

On that first morning, we went to the dining room together as soon as the intercom in our cabin announced that breakfast was being served. It was good to be able to stretch my legs after being cooped up for so long. And I felt extraordinarily light and buoyant because the *Susie*'s spin produced only one-third gravity, the same as surface gravity on Mars.

It's surprising when you stop to think of it that the spinning of a ship on its axis feels like gravity, not like *spin*. I mean, wouldn't you think that you'd know you were going round and round, and get dizzy? But you don't; you can't detect any motion at all. You can't tell any difference between the centrifugal force and real gravity. Of course, it's a little disconcerting to have the floor curve upward ahead of you, yet find it level when you get there. And the gravity isn't the same everywhere; it gets less as you go toward the center of the sphere. That's why the staterooms, dining room, and lounge are all next to the outer hull, with crew quarters and cargo space inboard. I had a general idea of the layout from what Alex had told me, though I'm sure I would have gotten lost if there hadn't been colored arrows on the wall pointing the way.

Dad was waiting for me near the entrance to the dining room; I introduced Janet, and we went in and found a table. I looked around but didn't see Alex anywhere. Pretty soon another woman joined us, since all the tables were for four.

"I don't suppose we're going to get very fancy meal service," Janet said.

As a matter of fact, the dining room was fixed up quite attractively, with an orange carpet and tabletops in a matching tone, and gold and beige fabric covering the walls. The chairs were comfortable, too, though they weren't upholstered; they didn't need to be, with the low gravity. What did she expect, crystal chandeliers? But I looked around, and the tables were jammed awfully close together, and the food did come all in one course—in compartmented trays instead of on china—and there wasn't any choice of menu. I said, "I guess we'd better get used to things being sort of primitive. They probably aren't any better on Mars."

Dad looked at me in a rather puzzled way, and I remembered

how careful I'd been to avoid telling him anything at all about what I expected of Mars. But when Janet commented, "The plumbing is certainly primitive enough," I found myself agreeing heartily.

"I don't think 'primitive' is the right word," said Dad. "Different from what you're used to, maybe. But it was a feat of very sophisticated engineering to fix things so that more than two hundred people can live for ten weeks in a self-contained environment like this."

"I guess so. But how long do they expect us to get along without any water to wash in? All I've had so far are those premoistened towel things." I remembered Alex's remark about getting used to water rationing, and went on, "Maybe to a Martian it doesn't matter, but—"

The other woman at our table, a Madame Duprés, interposed icily, "I think you'll find Martian cities considerably cleaner than cities on Earth." (She was right, by the way; because they're sealed and the air is manufactured, no dirt can get in.)

Well, of course I hadn't meant to imply that Martians weren't clean personally, only that they didn't see anything abnormal in having to make do with a limited supply of water. Somehow it hadn't come out right! My cheeks burned; the woman was probably another colonist and had thought I was insulting her. Whatever could I say?

I was saved by the ringing of a gong; everyone stopped talking and looked up to see a flight attendant standing on the dais at one end of the room, with a microphone in her hand. "Good morning, ladies and gentlemen. I hope that you've all enjoyed your breakfast, and that you had a comfortable night, though for some of you I know it was a short one—"

"Comfortable?" muttered Janet. "Who does she think she's kidding?"

The woman went on, "I'm Ms. Gonzalez, your head flight attendant. Right after this meal my staff and I will show you around the ship and explain some of the things you'll need to know. But first, I want to introduce the man you're all anxious to meet: Captain Bjornsen."

The captain got up and welcomed us, and then introduced other officers until I began to wonder who was piloting at the moment. One of the things he told us, though, was that the operation of the ship was largely automatic, and that the crew didn't have much to do until it came time to establish the orbit around Mars, except in case of emergency. It was certainly true that we saw a good deal of the officers all through the trip. People said, jokingly, that one reason they had so many of them on a spaceliner was so that the passengers would always have men and women in elegant uniforms to socialize with.

After everyone had finished eating, the flight attendants broke us up into small groups, by cabin numbers, for the Grand Tour. I wasn't in the same group as Dad, but since Janet was with me I didn't feel lonesome. And I didn't notice at all what a wet blanket Janet was. If I'd made that first tour with Alex, maybe I would have loved *Susie* from the start.

Do you know what life on a spaceliner is more like than anything else? Summer camp! I know that sounds ridiculous, because on the surface there don't seem to be many similarities. More adults than kids. (Though there are lots of kids, too, since practically all of the homesteaders have them.) No contact with nature at all.

But underneath there's a very close analogy. It's organized like camp. I didn't spot this at first, of course, but looking back I can see it. I only went to camp once, the summer I was fourteen, but it made a lasting impression on me, and some of the things that went on in the *Susie* were just the same.

To begin with, both in camp and aboard a spaceliner you're completely isolated from the outside. There you are, thrown with the same people day in and day out, with nobody coming or going; and a big camp's got just about the same number of people as the *Susie*, too. Naturally, on a ship you're a great deal more isolated than at camp, because you can't leave and you're millions of miles away from any other source of air, water, and food. That isolation, though, is precisely what makes adults willing to act like campers.

Next, there's the matter of obeying regulations. In camp those are enforced by the director, and on a spaceliner it's by the captain. He isn't like a military captain; he's aware that people are there because they've chosen to be, and that they expect to be given a chance to enjoy themselves. But in the last analysis, what he says goes. No arguments. No democratic votes. His decisions are all for the passengers' good, not his; but he doesn't stop to explain them.

If you have a problem, though, you don't try to see the captain about it. You talk to your flight attendant. And in some ways a flight attendant acts very much like a camp counselor. Don't think that she isn't there to supervise as well as to entertain; she is. If anyone needs supervising, she'll do it! She's responsible to the captain.

Some of the older people who were used to hotels and ocean cruises had to be straightened out about flight attendants; they thought they were supposed to tip them. That's not done, any more than it is on an airliner, even though you're aboard for weeks. (As a matter of fact, there's no tipping at all on Mars, and no Colonial appreciates a tip being offered.)

Anyway, as our tour guide started telling us what to expect aboard *Susie*, she was awfully reminiscent of a camp counselor with her little flock of charges and her list of points to be covered in first-day orientation. "Don't enter such-and-such an area without permission," "If you aren't feeling well report to the nurse," and so on. In both cases it's a separate little world whose smooth functioning—not to mention safety—depends on obedience to certain rules, and you have to be shown the ropes.

Another way in which a spaceliner's like camp is the way you get along without the comforts you have at home. For instance, our guide began by explaining about the drinking water; we'd be given a limited number of tokens a day for the automatic dispensing machines. Then she went on to describe the bath arrangements. There were the plastic-wrapped moistened towelettes for ordinary hands-and-face washing—much more sanitary than plain water anyway, she assured us—plus two sponge baths a week, for which we'd get tickets. Well, it's not that there's any shortage of water at camp (there, it could be something else basic, like electric lights), but the principle's the same. You find out that you don't need it as much as you thought you did.

The main thing that brought the summer camp idea into my mind, however, was the similarity of mealtime arrangements. In the first place, meals were stretched out to occupy as much time as possible. (There were four a day, following the British custom: afternoon tea as well as breakfast, lunch, and dinner.) Everyone ate together and waited until the last table was through, simply because it took longer that way. There were no regularly assigned tables; people were encouraged to mix differently each time, and the ship's officers tried to spread themselves around. Since the dining room was the only place in the ship big enough to accommodate everybody at once, all announcements were made at meals. But besides that, dinner was usually followed by community singing, just as if we were in the dining hall back at good old Camp Twin Firs! In the evening there'd often be a movie, or someone (usually a properly enthusiastic flight attendant) would organize impromptu skits. You wouldn't think that grown men and women, many of them scientists, would enter into that sort of thing. But they did, and I think most of them enjoyed it. It goes to show how customs really are the result of environment. Put people in the right situation, and they'll suspend all their old ideas about what's appropriate.

There weren't many organized activities during the daytime. Between meals, we could use the dining room to play cards, or just sit and talk, if the lounge was full. The lounge itself was small and was really meant for reading, music, and more or less private conversation. Most of it was broken up into small library cubicles, each with its own computer terminal. During the tour our flight attendant demonstrated how to enter the request for the book, recording, or game you wanted and download it to your handheld computer if you felt like taking it to your cabin; it was a standard setup except that it was based on physical media instead of being connected to the Net. That was startling, till we realized that interplanetary data channels have to be kept free for vital messages and even private mail is transmitted through official communications centers. Mars has its own Net, of course, but it's limited to local material and texts that have been physically imported.

The only other place to go in the *Susie,* aside from the children's playroom, was the gym. That was at the center of the passenger sphere, which meant that it was kept under zero gravity. The flight attendant explained that each morning there would be classes in zero-g acrobatics and asked how many of us were interested. I thought of how Alex had said this was fun and was about to volunteer, but I whispered to Janet first, "Are you going to?"

"Heavens, no!" she laughed. "Me? I'll keep my feet on the floor where they belong, thank you. Besides, I have studying to do."

I decided that probably she was right, it wouldn't be sensible. And hadn't I told Dad that I was going to start reading up on my basic college subjects during the trip? It would be foolish to waste such a good opportunity. So I didn't put up my hand.

At one end of the cylindrical gym was the observation bubble. There, at the axis of the ship, stars seemed to circle in the hazeless black sky, although actually it was the ship itself that was rotating. For the passengers' benefit *Susie* had been positioned to place the crescent Earth at the bubble's center. Ice blue and cloud-flecked, it waned as the ship spiraled outward from the sun.

We could pause only briefly since other tour groups were crowding up behind. The flight attendant shepherded us back through the gym, weightless, hand over hand along the guide rail. But I wanted a better look. "Let's come back later by ourselves, Janet," I suggested.

"It's hardly worth the trouble," she said. "We've seen plenty of pictures that were more effective. Earth will be smaller by then, and thinner."

As it happened, though, I did get back to the observation deck before Earth became a mere point of light, inestimably distant. I went that same evening, with Alex.

I didn't see Alex until dinner time. Janet and I were settling ourselves at a table near the door when suddenly he appeared beside me. "Hello, Melinda," he said. "How does *Susie* impress you so far?"

"Well, better than the original *Susan Constant*, anyway," I replied lightly. But as I said it, it suddenly struck me as being true. People who crossed the Atlantic in seventeenth-century sailing ships had a hard time of it. Usually they lived for weeks on end all jammed together in the hold, with no proper food or sanitation or anything; lots of them got sick and died.

"At least our ship's fairly sure to reach its destination," Alex said, smiling. "Theirs wasn't, not by any means."

That was true, too. It was taking us a shorter time to cross all these millions of miles than it had taken them to get from England to Virginia. And we even knew the exact day, hour, and minute that we'd arrive! "They had some unpredictable winds to contend with," I agreed.

"Not to mention a potential for being sunk."

"I don't know anything about any other *Susan Constant*," Janet said. "But if you're trying to say that it's guaranteed to be all fun and games on this one, I won't buy it."

Alex shook his head. "I wasn't saying that," he said soberly. "We all know better. But there's a certain parallel that's valid, I think. A certain indication that progress has been made since the sailing ship era."

"Progress for what, though?" I asked. "We may able to go to Mars in comparative safety and comfort, but who needs to?"

"Progress for science," Janet stated firmly. "That's the real value of the base on Mars. All this colonization business is one giant boondoggle, as far as I'm concerned."

Alex scowled at her. "I've heard that opinion before, of course; I spent a year on Earth." He hesitated, deciding how best to make his point. "You're both missing something. The settlement of Mars is the most important step forward the human race has ever made. But the scientific knowledge gained in the process is only incidental."

"Incidental?" sputtered Janet. "How can you say that? How else can you justify—"

"Please, let's not argue about it now," I begged, sorry that I'd ever raised the question. "Let's enjoy our dinner." I knew that

Alex's upbringing had affected his way of looking at things, and I didn't want to get back to the point where he was objecting to my natural assumptions again. I toyed nervously with my food, wishing that I'd chosen to eat with Dad.

But after the meal, when Alex asked me to walk to the observation deck with him, I didn't refuse. I couldn't, somehow. It was more than my wanting to look at Earth again; after all, if Janet wouldn't go with me, I probably could have prevailed upon Dad. I could have gone by myself, even. But the idea of going with Alex drew me; I couldn't help liking his company. Sometimes when I was talking to him my ideas seemed unsettled, inadequate, not at all well-organized the way they had been back at school. And I hated that feeling! But in spite of it there was something exciting—volatile, like weightlessness. A hint of something that I didn't quite want to ignore.

"I should have brought you your book," I said to him as we made our way through the gym toward the observation bubble.

"Read it first. I'm in no hurry." He turned to me, his gray eyes twinkling. "Or don't you like thrilling adventures?"

"Sure I do," I told him, though I didn't, especially. "At any rate, I enjoy reading about them."

"But not participating?" He laughed. "I shouldn't kid you. Here we are out in space, between planets; that would be more than enough adventure for lots of people. I don't know why I'm fascinated by wild tales of interstellar expeditions, and there's no reason why you should be."

We stood in silence for several minutes when we reached the viewport. Earth had shrunk to less than half the size it had been in the morning. The stars were brilliant, far more brilliant than I'd ever seen them at home. Over at one side of the bubble, shielded by darkened glass, were the fiery fringes of the sun.

"You look solemn again," Alex said finally. "Why, Melinda?"

"I was just thinking . . . fifty million miles."

He touched my arm. "More than that. Much more. We don't make a beeline, you know, even in a rush orbit. And if Mars were around on the other side of the sun—"

"It's not, is it?"

"Not at the moment. But don't think of interplanetary distances in miles if that bothers you. Think in terms of time. It's about the time from Spain to San Salvador, the year Columbus sailed."

"Doesn't it bother *you* at all? Do you enjoy looking out at it like this?"

"At the view? I never get tired of it; not after all the times I've seen stars from outside Earth's atmosphere."

"Janet Crane is very blasé about it."

"Janet is very blasé, period, from what little I've seen of her. You mustn't take her too seriously, Melinda."

"She isn't making any secret of the fact that she doesn't have a favorable opinion of the Colonies," I said. "But it's funny, I'd have thought she'd be a typical space enthusiast, as scientifically oriented as she is."

"There's not much connection."

"Isn't there? I've always thought a person would have to be completely wrapped up in science to leave Earth voluntarily."

"You don't know us Colonials very well, then. Lots of the people on Mars don't have any sort of scientific education. Take me, for example. I never had much aptitude for technical stuff, and I'd have made a pretty bad engineer. Besides, New Terrans aren't as single-minded as your roommate; we're primarily interested in *living*."

It was on the tip of my tongue to say, "Then why did you pick Mars to live on?" but I didn't. Instead I asked, "What did you enjoy most on Earth?"

Alex grinned at me. "Swimming, I think. Shower baths. And steak!"

That night as we were getting ready for bed Janet told me, "Well, anyway, I'm glad I'm rooming with you instead of one of those homesteaders! Honestly, Melinda, have you talked to any of them? They're absolutely out of their minds. Why the government wastes its money transporting those people to Mars to live, when it could be setting up more research centers, increasing scientific grants—"

"I'm sure the Colonies must be of some benefit."

"I'm not. What possible use is colonization? Any first-year biology student can tell you that terrestrial life-forms can never adapt to Mars. The environment is just too hostile."

"They seem to be doing all right. Alex Preston, the man who sat with us at dinner, is a second-generation Martian, and it seems—well, almost normal to him."

"Is that who you spent the evening with?" she asked curiously.

"Yes. I think he's nice."

"Nice enough, I guess. But after all, he's a Colonial." Giving me a sisterly look, she added sharply, "Melinda, I do hope you aren't interested in him."

"Of course I'm not," I told her. "Not that way." Because her tone had left no doubt as to which way she meant. It hadn't even occurred to me, and I was shocked. I realized that perhaps I had better try to avoid Alex, when I could. He *was* a Colonial, and he and I couldn't really have anything in common.

More than that, I didn't want anything in common with anyone except Ross. Certainly not a shipboard romance!

I lay back on my narrow bunk, closed my eyes, and tried to concentrate on a picture of the green fir tree towering outside my bedroom window at Gran's. The atmosphere of the *Susie* was suddenly stifling; I would gladly have jumped out into the vacuum of space if it could have gotten me back to the cool, free air of Maple Beach. At that moment, I was sure that the coming ten weeks were going to be the longest that I had ever spent.

Chapter 7

The days fell into a pattern, and in spite of my resolution Alex was part of the pattern. I couldn't turn away from him without being downright rude; and though I tried to avoid him, I didn't actually want to. Besides, there weren't many single people on the ship, and so Alex and I just naturally spent much of our time in each other's company.

My pattern at school had been to do everything with my roommates when I wasn't out with Ross, and so aboard *Susie* I expected to go around with Janet. I admired her immensely; she was so cool, so smart, so sure of herself! And out of all the people on the ship with whom she might have made friends, she seemed to prefer my companionship. She liked me, I think, because I agreed with her. Anyway, I thought I agreed with her, and if there were things in Janet's way of thinking that disturbed me at all, I never gave them any consideration.

Our feelings toward Mars were not popular. The others on the ship were homesteaders who had given up everything else in their lives in order to emigrate, or else they were men and women who'd won out over a lot of competition in order to be sent to the Colonies to work. They did not understand anyone who didn't think Mars was the greatest planet in the universe! Such a lack of understanding was by no means one-sided, for Janet and I had no comprehension at all of their viewpoint. Janet was very frank in expressing her opinions. I wasn't, because of my shyness, though as time went on I followed her lead with less and less reluctance.

However, Janet and I saw each other mainly in our stateroom, for she spent much of her time in study. She'd brought plenty of e-files dealing with extraterrestrial biology to supplement those the ship's library had, and so from after breakfast until bedtime I was often left at loose ends.

I intended to study too, so that I'd be able to qualify for advanced standing in some of my college subjects, but I didn't accomplish much. I didn't know how to go at it. I had no college reading lists yet, and the library didn't contain basic texts other than ones on subjects related to Mars, which weren't relevant. In any case, there was a time limit on the library booths and I wasn't used to reading much on the small screen of my handheld computer; our rooms at school had been equipped with desktop screens. When I'd covered the history selections—superficially, I'll admit, for somehow I couldn't concentrate well enough to actually *study* them—I came to a not-too-reluctant standstill.

You may well ask why I didn't spend more time with Dad, since that was the whole point of the trip in the first place. Well, it just never seemed to come off, that's all. There wasn't anything we could do together. We exhausted what we had to say to each other merely by sitting at the same table for one or two meals a day. We'd been apart too long; we were strangers and didn't have enough mutual interests. Poor Dad, he *wanted* to reach me. I wanted, desperately, to reach him. I'd sit there trying to come up with something to say, and I'd just freeze; I never have been good at small talk. Until those weeks aboard *Susie*, I hadn't known that I'd inherited this characteristic from him.

Of course, Dad had studying to do, too: e-files of material on the firm's proposed Martian operations, with which he'd have to be thoroughly familiar in order to make effective use of his time there. And he'd found friends in his own field. So at first we made elaborate excuses, and then after a while we just accepted the fact that we'd meet daily for breakfast, and that would be it.

If it hadn't been for Alex, I would have been terribly lonely. I'd be sitting in the lounge and Alex would come along, and we'd talk. Or sometimes we'd be asked to play bridge; before long a tournament got going and we joined that, as partners. It was a very effective time consumer. There was also a chess tournament, but though Alex taught me to play I didn't try it often; the others on board were experienced, and much too good for me. I did watch a lot. Alex himself was an expert and had climbed to third place before the trip was over.

Then, too, after the first week or so we went to the gym fairly frequently; when I found that I wouldn't be seeing much of Janet, I changed my mind about not joining the classes. Alex helped me pass the zero-g test for my card, and he was right, it *was* fun! Once I'd learned to relax and simply float, it was marvelous. At first, though, I was so nervous and tense that I just couldn't get the hang of it. I'd close my eyes, and it would feel like an elevator out of control, and I'd want to get out of there! Finally Alex got stern with me and made me let go.

"Look, Mel," he said. "It's new and it's different, sure. You're fighting it, that's why you thrash around that way. Relax. Relax and enjoy it!" Eventually I did; that was all it took. Before long I didn't even need the antinausea shots.

In the evening, we participated in whatever was planned. We sat together for movies; we were roped into some silly skit one night and were runners-up for the booby prize; side by side, we joined in the singing of the old songs. songs that were popular long before the spaceship *Susan Constant* ever set forth on a wider sea than any known to the sailors who originated them: "The Mermaid," "Blow the Man Down," "Shenandoah." On the night of the midcrossing party, we even danced (normally there wasn't room, but they piled the tables up, easy enough to do in one-third gravity, to clear the space). But it wasn't like dating. We were friendly, never more than that; we didn't even hold hands. I didn't feel that I was doing anything that Ross could object to.

I never got too well acquainted with any of the homesteaders. In the first place, they were all married couples, older than I was and absorbed by their careers as well as by their accustomed social pattern. Yet the big thing that separated us was not the difference in our ages and interests, but the wide gulf in our attitudes. Particularly our attitudes about Mars. The surprising thing was that the gulf was just as wide between Alex and me, if not wider; yet with Alex, it wasn't the same kind of barrier. It was never mentioned between us any more than it was mentioned between me and Dad. Alex simply went on talking about

Mars in a casual way that seemed more a sincere pride in the Colonies than a deliberate attempt to convert me.

If he was making an effort, it didn't succeed. Because, though I enjoyed listening to Alex, I enjoyed it in the same way a person might enjoy hearing someone tell about the inhabitants of some other solar system—she'd be interested, but she wouldn't think of it as real life. Or at any rate she wouldn't connect it with her own life. It would remain foreign and exotic to her even if it were factual. I imagine many Americans once thought of Africa and Asia in the same way. Alex could just as well have been an anthropologist describing tribal cultures, for all I connected the things he told me with *him*, as a person.

I remember once, over tea one afternoon, he mentioned that he had been almost ten years old before he had gone Outside— outside the domes, that is. My reaction was, "Didn't you feel imprisoned all those years, before? I can't imagine little boys on Earth being penned up like that."

He laughed. "You must have a funny idea of what our cities are like. Sure, I looked forward to going Outside, just as you probably looked forward to a vacation at the beach. But I had plenty of chances around home to get into mischief, and I took full advantage of them. Kids on Mars act just the same as they do anyplace else."

One of the things more permissible in the social climate of the *Susie* than under ordinary circumstances was serious discussion, and the significance of space exploration was an inexhaustible topic. The talk seemed to get around to it whenever a group gathered. It was all rather over my head, but Alex thoroughly enjoyed it. And he took it as seriously as some people do bridge scores; at times he got really angry. Of course Alex was something of a fanatic on the subject, as most Colonials are.

I remember one evening in particular, when we were sitting around after dinner, finishing our coffee. Dad happened to be with us, as well as an older man, a Professor Goldberg who was on his way to spend a sabbatical at the University of Mars. We were discussing a letter to the editor that had appeared in the *Interplanetary Observer*, one of the current magazines beamed out to us from Earth, which Dad had happened to read and was summarizing for the professor. Down at the other end of the dining room a bunch of the homesteaders were singing; someone had found a guitar among *Susie's* recreational supplies, and we could hardly hear ourselves talk.

"Anyway," Dad shouted, "this fellow wound up with the old 'we had better solve all the problems on this world before we take a chance on messing up any others' line."

"That makes me furious!" Alex yelled back. "Of all the mistaken theories about space that I ran into on Earth, that's the most shortsighted."

"Why?" I ventured. "It sounds logical enough to me."

All three of them jumped on me as if I'd just come out in favor of slavery. "Mel, honey, you just haven't gone into it," Dad began, but Alex said rather sharply, "With your interest in history I should think you could see the fallacy easily enough."

"In the first place," Professor Goldberg said, "we can't ever solve all the problems on Earth. We're human. We can make progress—we *have* made progress: Peace is better assured than it was a hundred years ago; the standard of living has risen all over the world; racial equality is a reality now, and freedom for the individual is more widespread than it was in the twentieth century—"

"It was the conquest of space that helped to bring about peace," Alex interrupted. "Energy went into that which would otherwise have gone into war."

Like in the poem, I thought. *Nightmare, endless wars . . . then we turned spaceward.*

"More than that, though," the professor went on, "for the human race to stay cooped up on one world would lead only to a terrible sort of stagnation. It would create problems, not solve them."

"Stagnation or something worse," said Alex darkly, "with the population situation the way it is. Without a frontier for expansion, neither today's living standard nor freedom could last— and there'd eventually be violence."

"I really don't think that we need to worry too much about that anymore, though," said the professor. "The Colonies are well established now."

"Yes, but there's this new debate over the appropriation coming up," Alex said. "Someday we'll be self-sufficient, but now—"

"I forget, you Colonials are a bit sensitive on that subject," the professor replied. "Still, I don't think the ultimate fate of colonization is in much danger. Think how much opposition there was initially, yet that didn't stop people. It won't stop the next step, either—the stars."

"Human beings won't ever be stopped from moving on," Alex said firmly. "The need for challenge, for seeing what's over the hill—it's built in. It's a fact of nature."

Dad turned to me. "Your mother once said something like that, Mel. She told me, 'My ancestors crossed the plains in a covered wagon. The woman in the family, Melinda, didn't want to go, but her husband, Jess, said that he aimed to see the Oregon Country and nobody was going to stop him. Jess believed that since God put Oregon there, it must be in the nature of people to want to see it."

I was silent, sipping my coffee. Was that true, that my ancestor Melinda Stillwell had to be talked into going west? How little I really knew about her!

The group of homesteaders clustered around the guitar player was still holding forth with one song after another, rousing songs from old-time musicals like *Oklahoma!*, *My Fair Lady*, and *Paint Your Wagon*. The current melody was one I'd always loved:

> *I was born under a wanderin' star,*
> *I was born under a wanderin' star.*
> *Staying put can kill you,*
> *Standing still's a curse,*
> *To settle down can drive you mad*
> *But moving on is worse.*
> *I was born under a wanderin' star. . . .*

Alex said, "In the nineteenth century they called it 'Manifest Destiny.' I know that term was often used politically, in a nationalistic sense. But there was more to it than that."

"Much more," the professor agreed. "It fired people's imaginations, and the reason it did was that underneath, there was an idea there that had nothing to do with nationalism—an idea that was valid. The idea that the human race *will* keep on moving, that we've got to expand or perish."

I could scarcely hear him, what with the volume of the chorus:

> *Aching for to stop and always aching for to go;*
> *Searching, but for what I never will know.*
> *I was born under a wanderin' star,*
> *A wanderin' . . . wanderin' star.*

The conversation drifted on to other things, then; but it set me to thinking. The colonists' viewpoint might not be as silly as I had believed.

But if my mind was opening a little, Janet's wasn't, and she was getting a reputation around the ship that I didn't thoroughly see the reason for. Nobody could expect every person to be overjoyed at the prospect of spending some time on Mars. Why wasn't she just as much entitled to her opinion as anyone else?

I said this to Alex once, and his reaction surprised me. "Melinda," he said seriously, "would you be offended by a piece of advice from old Uncle Alex here?"

"Of course not."

"Don't stay too close to Janet, then. You can't help seeing her often while you're sharing a room with her, but she's not exactly the person I'd pick for a role model."

"I don't think you're being fair to Janet," I protested. "Just because she doesn't see eye to eye with you about Mars—"

"It's not that. It's the superior way she acts, as if she knows everything there is to know, and what's more, as if everything Martian must be slightly inferior to its Terrestrial counterpart. She won't win many friends by it in the Colonies, and neither will you."

"I don't think I know everything!" I bristled. "And I'm perfectly aware that Colonials aren't inferior to anyone."

"But *different?*"

"Yes, of course, different; they'd have to be, to—"

"You see what I mean."

"No, I don't see," I said. "Look, the life people lead on Mars may seem normal enough to you because you were there before you saw Earth, but it doesn't to me, and I just can't look at it any other way."

"I know you can't, now. I hope someday you'll change your mind. But whether you do or not, why not give us Martians the benefit of the doubt? Give us credit for being human, anyway!"

Indignantly I demanded, "Now who's acting superior?" Alex did sound like an uncle sometimes! He was only a few years older than I was, but he'd grown up too fast; people did, I supposed, in the Colonies.

"Sorry," he said. "It's just a suggestion. Don't start off on the wrong foot, Melinda. You're too nice a girl."

I thought about that conversation a good deal after it was over with. In spite of my having assured Alex that I wouldn't be offended by his advice, it bothered me. I had thought it was I who was keeping the distance, because of Ross, because of—well, a lot of things. It was somehow upsetting to feel that Alex might not really like me, that in some ways I might not measure up to his standards.

We were almost two months out when a thing happened that crystallized the fear I'd so far been denying. It was a perfectly ordinary afternoon; we were in the middle of a bridge game. All of a sudden a rhythmic, raucous squawk began to come out of the intercom speakers. Back at the beginning of the trip we had been told what to do if an alarm sounded—all passengers were to gather in the dining room, where Alex and I already were. But I hadn't imagined it really happening. As the incessant bleating continued, icy tentacles slid up my spine and clutched at the base of my mind.

The couple we were playing with, a young doctor from India and his bride, moved their chairs together; he put his arm around her. She looked at him with big, luminous eyes and asked what I had not dared to put into words: "Have we been hit by a meteor?"

Her husband didn't know what to say. But Alex told us calmly, "It's probably more or less of a drill. Sometimes there's a hit, too small to be dangerous, but the automatic alarm system picks it up and they go through with the alert on general principles."

He smiled at me. "Can't disillusion the public about space travel being exciting, you know."

That was exactly what had happened; before long the captain came in and assured us that there was nothing to worry over. The hole wasn't big enough for there to be any hurry about patching it, and no pressure had been lost. He apologized for putting us through the drill, but explained that it was necessary to keep in practice in case there ever was a real emergency.

That was that; the passengers who'd been busy elsewhere drifted out, and we went on to finish the game. But later, when I went to my cabin to dress for dinner, I found Janet lying on her bunk, doing nothing, with an abnormally blank and frozen look.

"Why, what's the matter?" I asked. "Aren't you feeling well, Janet? Should I call the nurse?"

She turned on me in fury. "I hate it!" she choked. "It's not right that a person should have to risk her life to establish her professional standing! I know just as much about extraterrestrial microbes from studying texts as I'll ever learn on Mars—there's no life to speak of on Mars anyway. Why should the University of Mars be the only place to work with specimens from the outer planets, when everybody knows that Earth's quarantine laws are archaic? I wish I hadn't come; I wish I'd told them I wouldn't do it and made them waive that stupid requirement. I wish we'd never even discovered Mars!" Unaccountably, she began to sob.

I stared at her. This wasn't like Janet, not at all. She was so self-assured, usually. Then I realized what the trouble was. Janet

was scared! Underneath that icy exterior, she was absolutely terrified.

I felt sick. So I wasn't the only one. Janet, with all her experience, her scientific training, was as awed by space as I was. More
so, even; her fright wasn't the same as the vague fears that I'd so
far managed to talk myself out of. Janet knew—or thought she
knew—something specific.

I sat down on the edge of the bunk and gripped her shoulders.
"Janet, what is it? What's happened?"

Her face was red and distorted from crying, and she didn't
stop shaking. "Don't you know? Don't you know what that meteor alarm business was all about?"

"Alex said it was just standard procedure, a drill."

"Well, of course *he* would. When will you learn that those id-
iots won't ever admit how foolish and dangerous the whole thing
is? Grow up, Melinda!"

I thought it over. He had admitted one thing, perhaps, the
very first day. Janet had said, "Are you trying to tell us that it's
guaranteed to be all fun and games aboard this ship?" And Alex
had answered, "I'm not saying that . . . *we all know better.*" I
hadn't thought anything of it. With all my doubts, I hadn't
imagined that we were facing a calculated danger.

"It's just one gigantic gamble," Janet was saying. "The fact
that there hasn't been a major disaster on a spaceliner yet makes
it all the worse; the chances are increasing. It's not reasonable to
think that ship after ship can go all these millions of miles without being struck by anything big, or that the domes on Mars can
stand indefinitely, either. Think how many craters there are on

Mars! Government officials won't admit how worried they are, and naturally TPC won't. The colonists have their heads in the sand. But sooner or later something's going to happen. It's like earthquakes—you can live right on top of a fault for years, but eventually—"

"But Janet," I protested, more concerned with convincing myself than with comforting her. "Janet, surely the chances of our being hit by anything big enough to do any real harm are pretty slight. There's never been a ship damaged before."

"That's exactly why they think the time's getting closer." (She didn't specify who *they* were.)

"Maybe so, but why should we think—"

"Because we've run into a swarm of them, that's why! What other reason could they have for a drill so near the end of the trip? Sure, the last meteor was small, but—" She looked at me, her eyes dark. "It wouldn't even have to hit the passenger decks. The oxygen tanks would be even worse. Or the fuel supply, or the engines—we'd go right on past Mars, out into space *forever.* Do you know what would happen if a ship ran low on air, Melinda?"

"I—I never thought about it."

"They'd draw lots. It's all set forth in the regulations, the ones they don't publicize."

"I don't understand."

"Because the air would last twice as long for half as many people, of course. The captain's sworn to enforce it."

It never occurred to me to ask her how she knew; I now suspect that this last bit of "information" came from some overdramatized TV series. But at the time, all I could think of was, *Three weeks. If we can just get through the next three weeks—* And then I remembered that the domes on Mars were vulnerable, too.

There is something particularly terrifying about the concept of lack of air. It's so alien to your experience on Earth that you just can't take it seriously at first. But when the idea gets through, it really throws you. Have you ever gone underwater without having a chance to fill your lungs first? Or been so exhausted from running that you couldn't get your breath? In those situations there *is* air; you aren't frightened, because you know those agonizing sensations will be gone in a few moments. But to be without air, to feel it rushing away through some deadly gap in a fragile shell, dispersing into nothingness, and to know that there's no way it can be replaced. . . . Once I began to picture it, I was horror-stricken.

What I should have done was to discuss the whole thing with Dad. Dad had been an engineer, and though he wasn't an expert on space, he undoubtedly knew a great deal more about it than Janet did, besides having more common sense! But you always tend to believe the worst of a situation, at least I always do, and somehow I got the idea into my head that the facts would upset Dad and that I ought not to burden him with them. I completely overlooked the likelihood that he would never have brought me aboard in the first place if the danger were anywhere near as great as Janet imagined.

So I went on worrying over it, all alone. I didn't tell Alex, and at least I had sense enough not to spread it any further; instinctively I knew that rumors can mean trouble aboard a ship. Janet didn't talk to anyone else, either, for she was too ashamed of the crack in her composure. We didn't even mention it between ourselves again.

But it bothered me—bothered me more and more as time went on, instead of the reverse. I began counting the days, not until arrival on Mars, but until our scheduled return to Earth eight months in the future. Much of the time I was acutely conscious of each indrawn breath. Air . . . life . . . so scant within the ship, the only other source so incredibly remote! More than once I had a nightmare in which a gaping hole appeared in the floor between my feet and I was left gasping, spinning with bursting lungs toward a faint spark in the blackness that fell . . . and fell. . . .

Maybe it wasn't entirely the result of my exaggerated physical fears. Maybe there was more symbolism to it than that; they say there are symbols behind everything. I wouldn't have admitted it then, but underneath I must have been aware that what really frightened me wasn't the unlikely possibility that *Susie's* strong metal hull would be penetrated. The thought of what might lie outside the narrow, safe pattern I'd drawn for my life was more dismaying than all the empty void through which the *Susan Constant* was hurtling.

Part Three
MARS

Chapter 8

I first saw Mars from the observation bubble of the *Susan Constant*. Oh, I'd seen it from Earth, I suppose, but I never paid any attention to it then. On Earth, it's difficult to think of Mars as a place, that tiny reddish star—well, not a star, of course, but in the sky it looks like one. It's impossible to believe that such a tiny point of light can be the focus of people's lives and people's dreams.

As soon as we got close enough to see Mars as a disk, the captain turned *Susie* so that the observation bubble faced it and announced that people could go and look. Immediately there was a big rush; the homesteaders could hardly wait to get a glimpse of their new world. I wasn't in any particular hurry, but Alex was, so we stood in line with everyone else.

At that time, the only feature we could make out was the glittering south polar cap, which happened to be at its largest. As the days passed, though, dark patches began to appear against the reddish face of the globe, splotches that Alex identified for me with pride, just as I might have pointed out North America to him if I'd been with him when he approached Earth for the first time. Syrtis Major was the most prominent, a conspicuous triangle. But there were others: Sinus Meridiani, Solis Lacus, Aurorae Sinus. . . . How foolishly romantic the old astronomers were! Utopia, Eden, the Fountain of Youth, the Sea of Pearls. I wonder what they would think if they could take a close look at some of the drab, uninteresting places they christened, and hear those idealized names in everyday use.

The names are doubly inappropriate, for Mars doesn't have seas and continents, as those astronomers thought when the naming was done. A *mare, sinus,* or *lacus* is, when you get to it, a section of dry land—very dry—and not really dark, either, except by comparison. All in all, it's a barren, dried-up wasteland of a world, at least it seemed so to me as I looked at it from space. To Alex it was beautiful! "Glowing," "rich," and "vivid" were some of the words he used. I had never really believed before that beauty is in the eye of the beholder.

On the last night out there was a party. Almost everyone was in an exuberant mood; the discussion was noisier than usual, the singing louder, and the entertainment more nonsensical. The festivities showed no signs of breaking up by midnight, though the ship's officers disappeared early for once. Finally I excused myself and went to bed.

I was torn two ways. On one hand, it was a tremendous relief to think that I'd soon be safely out of space and onto solid land; but on the other, I wasn't looking forward to adjusting all over again. *Susie* might have her drawbacks, but she was a nice little world in a sense. On board I knew what to expect, at any rate. And besides, there was Alex.

I would miss him! I hadn't thought before how I'd miss him.

When you see a person every day for ten weeks—spend half your waking hours with that person, in fact—why, it's something of a shock to realize that you aren't going to be doing it anymore. Even if he's just a casual friend and you're in love with someone else, the idea's a depressing one.

Naturally I would see him again. He had already invited Dad and me to have dinner at his home, with his parents; and Dad would undoubtedly reciprocate by taking us all out to a restaurant some night soon. But we wouldn't have the constant, easy companionship we'd had aboard the ship. And I couldn't go out with Alex even if he should ask me; that would be dating. Ross wouldn't want me to, though Alex and I were only friends.

In the morning after breakfast we were sent to our cabins and told to strap down. Zero-g was nothing strange to me anymore; I'd been to the gym too often. What was odd was to have "up" and "down" shift within the cabin as power was applied. Strapped to my bunk, I wasn't thrown around, and no high acceleration was used. But I was glad when the maneuvers were over and we were weightless again, in a stable parking orbit high above the surface of Mars.

Disembarkation was alphabetical, and "Ashley" being near the top of the list, Dad and I went down on the first shuttle. Alex came to the vestibule to see us off. "Mel, I—I want you to keep this," he said to me. "For a souvenir."

"But I already have souvenirs," I began, thinking of the little scrolls that had been distributed at the party the night before as well as of the digital snapshots that we'd all stored on our memory cards at one ship's function or another.

"This is just something between the two of us." He thrust it out to me, smiling. "It's all I have to give you, here, and I'm afraid it doesn't exactly suit your taste. But maybe it will remind you of the trip."

It was the book I'd brought on board for him that first day, a novel that I'd long since read and returned. But he'd written inside, "To Melinda, my fellow adventurer," and then "S.S. *Susan Constant*," the date, and his signature. By that, he'd turned it into a thing that I would treasure.

"Thank you, Alex," I said, wishing it didn't sound so flat.

"There's only one sort of thanks I want," he told me. "Give my planet a chance! Don't go down there bound and determined to hate everything."

"Oh, Alex, I'll try."

"Don't *try*. Just relax and enjoy it. Like zero-g, remember?" He gripped my hands between his strong ones. "Good-bye for now, Melinda."

There are two colonies on Mars so far: Marsport, in the southern hemisphere, which is solely a government-sponsored experimental project, and New Terra. The latter is by far the largest and is the only place open to homesteading, so it was where practically all of *Susie*'s passengers were bound.

The shuttle was a near duplicate of the one we'd come up from Earth to the *Susie* on, but we were aboard less than three hours. Mars hovered above us on the TV screen, ruddy and swollen, until at some undefinable moment it became less a whole planet and more a broad surface. From the looks of things we were going to crash *up* into it; it already seemed to be crushing us. In actuality, what was happening was that the ship had been turned on its tail, and the braking rockets were blasting away with a full g of deceleration. That being more gravity than I'd felt for a long time, it seemed worse than the liftoff from Earth.

I don't know what I had expected of the spaceport. Certainly not a terminal just like the one at Canaveral! Well, it wasn't exactly like it, for it was much smaller, and naturally it was pressurized, though that didn't show. Then too, there was much less bustle. But, except for being light on my feet, I might have been in any underground terminal on Earth.

We didn't stay there long; we were herded directly to the monorail for the ride into the city. The loading chamber was underground, but before we'd got up much speed we saw daylight ahead and broke out onto the surface of Mars.

You can imagine a thing, and see pictures of it, and still not have any conception of it at all. I'd heard countless times that the Martian ground is red. But what does *red* mean? Brick-red, scarlet, rust-colored, vermilion? It's all of those and more—the sand and the rocks both, the cliffs and the rippling hills. Rising out of all this redness, on the other side of a small crater, we could see the domes of New Terra, iridescent half spheres sparkling against the pinkish veil of the sky.

I had never thought there would be such a lot of domes! They looked as ephemeral as a cluster of soap bubbles, and as fragile. Actually, I knew, they were made of tough plastic, supported by air pressure from inside, and were in no danger at all of either collapsing or floating away. They could undoubtedly be punctured, though; a fair-sized meteor, for instance . . . I shivered. The same old thing again! For a moment or two I'd been overcome by the startling splendor of the scene; I'd forgotten what an unnatural sort of beauty it was.

A sudden burst of desperation made me uncomfortably aware of breathing again, and I moved back from the window. Canned air. Manufactured, imprisoned air; not only on the ship, but in the terminal, the monorail car, and in those deceptively lovely domes. And all around us, weird rolling landscapes where human beings could never walk without protection. It was a relief to plunge underground again, and to get out of the car into a perfectly ordinary-looking subway depot.

New Terra has two hotels: the Champs-Elysées, which is run by TPC under contract to Earth's government, and the newer Mars Hilton. Dad and I were booked at the Hilton; our reservation had of course been confirmed before our visas were issued. (It would be a sad state of affairs for anyone to arrive on Mars without a place to sleep, and the Colonial authorities see to it that it doesn't happen.) Our suite consisted of two tiny bedroom compartments with a sitting room between that wasn't much larger. What with doors on three of its walls and the TV screen on the fourth, there wasn't room for a window, but very few New Terran buildings have windows in any case, even on the floors above ground. Artificial lighting's needed whether or not the rooms get any of the dome-filtered daylight; and if they don't face on a mall, there wouldn't be any view.

It was only a little after seventeen o'clock in New Terra (the Martian day is practically the same length as the terrestrial one—an extra minute and a half in each hour—and we left our watches at the hotel desk to be adjusted.) But we were both tired and ready for bed; after all, we'd had dinner hours earlier, before boarding the shuttle. I picked up my duffel bag, which though I was used to one-third gravity seemed startlingly easy to lift, and headed for my own compartment with the briefest of good-nights to Dad.

The compartment was such an improvement over my cabin on the *Susie* that its size didn't faze me at first glance, but as I arranged my things I couldn't help but think wistfully of a less encouraging contrast. If I were at Gran's there'd be a window to open; the breeze would sweep in, fluttering the curtains and carrying with it the sound and smell of the sea. . . .

It seemed funny not to have said good night to Alex. Usually we'd been together until just before going to our cabins. But how silly! What a ridiculous thing to be bothered about, my first night on Mars.

I was bound to get over the feeling in a few days. Why, even missing Ross hadn't loomed too large in my mind during the past weeks. Had I ever really missed Ross? I thought suddenly. Earth, the old routine, certainly I'd missed those terribly. I'd lain awake in that cramped upper berth and longed desperately to be back there; I'd shed a good many tears over it, in fact. But how long had it been since I'd even pictured Ross's face? When I was homesick, it was less for Ross than for Maple Beach. How strange, when I'd always heard that people in love dream constantly of each other!

Of course, I'd been preoccupied; lately that awful, nagging

fear had been absorbing all the emotion I could get up. Yet having arrived on Mars, why should I be less concerned about missing Ross than about missing Alex?

I slipped on my robe and went back to the sitting room, determined to write to Ross right away. Hardly anyone had written letters on the ship because transmission back to Earth was too expensive. In New Terra, though, the data-link facilities were more powerful, and I could probably afford to send one every week or so. Ross might have written to me already; why, I wondered, hadn't I thought to check as soon as we arrived?

Picking up my handheld computer, I searched for the plug-in to the local Net, wondering whether it was linked to the TV screen or if I'd be stuck with my tiny one throughout our stay. Just then the door to Dad's compartment opened and he called out, "Everything okay, Mel, honey?"

"Yes. I'm worn out, but I'm not sleepy." He didn't close the door, and after a minute or two I went on, "Dad?"

"Yes, honey?"

"Is 'absence makes the heart grow fonder' true?"

Dad came over and stood beside me, his hands on my shoulders. "That depends on how much in love you are, I guess. With your mother and me it was always true."

"Even before you were married?"

"Especially then."

"Did you miss Mother when you weren't with her? Did you think about her much?"

"All the time!" He smiled, remembering. "Finally I knew I couldn't do justice to my job without giving more attention to it, so I gave up the field bonus, and went back and married her. She wouldn't let me turn down the next site I was offered; she went with me instead. Peru, it was. That was the year before you were born."

What was wrong with me? I thought. How could I not feel that way? Would I move to Peru to be with Ross? Or suppose he had wanted to homestead on Mars, as Dad once had—but that was impossible to imagine, because Ross *wouldn't*.

The next morning I was awakened by Dad's voice, talking to someone on the phone. I couldn't hear what he was saying; I lay there, not wanting to get out of bed and face the day, until he knocked on my door and called, "Come on, honey. We're invited out to breakfast."

Immediately I was wide awake. Alex had called much sooner than I'd thought he would! It must be Alex; after all, we didn't know anyone else that well.

But it wasn't. It was the president of the chamber of commerce. It seemed that he and his wife were anxious to show Dad and me around the city, starting right away. While I was puzzling over that, Dad remarked, "Better get out your fanciest dress for tonight, honey. We're going to a dinner party at the governor's."

I dropped my hairbrush. "The *governor*? Do you know him, Dad?"

"No, but he's very much interested in having my company open a branch here, you know."

Well, I hadn't known; or at any rate I hadn't stopped to think. The last thing I wanted was to go to a formal dinner and have to talk to all those dignitaries. The dinners Ross's mother had given had been bad enough. I'd dreaded them, but sometimes Mr. and Ms. Franklin had wanted their son to be present when they entertained, and I'd had no choice but to attend as his date. Often there had been important businessmen there, and Ross had been anxious for me to make a good impression; but I'd never been able to open my mouth. The food always tasted like so much sawdust to me on those occasions.

This was hardly the problem I'd expected to be confronted with on my first day in the Colonies. And what was worse, I didn't have a single thing to wear to such an affair; all I'd brought, besides my tired-looking travel suit, were school clothes. Moreover, I'd already observed that Colonial styles weren't a bit like styles at home. Women in the subway and hotel lobby had been wearing either shorts or skirts that weren't much longer; no one had on regular pants. (I had to admit that however impractical a style this might have been in cold climates, it was suitable for the steady seventy-two-degree climate of New Terra's domes.) Dad was no help; he seemed to think I should never have gotten into such a fix.

"Mel, honey, if you needed clothes, why didn't you tell me before we left?" he said impatiently. "I'd have given you money if you'd asked for it. If Portland stores didn't stock Colonial styles, Orlando's would have. Of course, I don't know much about these things—"

He'd known enough to come prepared himself, with shorts and jackets that would have looked like something out of a musical comedy at home, I noticed. I shook my head. "It wasn't the money," I said. "It just never occurred to me. I knew I wouldn't be dating, and I never thought about being invited out with you. Look, I'll just stay here tonight, Dad. I'd rather, really I would."

"Nonsense. Certainly you won't; you can't stay in the hotel for the next five months. Besides, there are some social obligations attached to the kind of business I'll be doing, Mel. That's one reason the firm agreed to send you in your mother's place. Put on your travel suit for now, and we'll try to get you a dinner dress this afternoon."

Mr. and Ms. Ortega from the chamber of commerce met us in the hotel restaurant and treated us to a typical Colonial breakfast: cereal, muffins, tomatoes, and ham. Things like the butter, sugar, and coffee were obviously synthetic, and I could see they'd take some getting used to. The cereal and muffins were passable, though not exactly like those at home, and the tomatoes were fresh. I didn't dare ask what the "ham" was made of.

The oddest thing about New Terra, the thing that hit me right away, was the absence of vehicles. (Cars aren't needed in the domes; people actually get around faster than in a regular city, because the subway's efficient and walking's not much of an effort under the low gravity.) It was nice to see gardens full of familiar, imported flowers where I'd normally expect streets, though I knew they were there as much to help take carbon dioxide out of the air as for aesthetic purposes. But something was missing. In spite of crowds New Terra seemed empty. Nothing I could define clearly—just a certain, well, alienness. Perhaps the trace of antiseptic in the air, or the raw cleanness of the place, as though it had been newly dusted. And it wasn't a free sort of emptiness. On the top level the sky showed through the translucence of the dome, but it didn't look real, somehow; it was unchanging, like a painted cyclorama.

The Hilton, where we started out that day, is near the center of New Terra's largest dome; its front door opens onto the big central plaza called the Etoile, from which all the malls radiate. The main mall is, naturally, the Champs-Elysées, and it's distinguished not only by the hotel of the same name, but by the city hall. None of the buildings looked very big to me, but I found that they're like icebergs; there's more to them below than above. In fact, they're normally entered from below, directly from the subway.

I was rather depressed by the residential districts, although I knew it wouldn't be practical to pressurize acres and acres of space just so everyone could have a real house and yard. Apartments are much more economical—after all, there's the cost not only of land, but of air. And I had to admit that they weren't bad-looking apartments, with their roof gardens and all. Lots of people live in apartments on Earth, by choice. Only they *have* a choice.

"What kind of houses do people on the homesteads have?" I asked Ms. Ortega.

"Homesteads? My dear, you have the wrong impression. There aren't any homesteads like in the old American West. The homesteaders live right here; most of us are homesteaders, or our parents were."

"But I thought the whole idea of homesteading was to give people free land."

"It started that way. But undomed land isn't any good. We do retain an option to claim acreage Outside, but it's worthless until somebody discovers a use for it. Basically, homesteaders' rights mean title to an apartment and a share in the farm."

"You mean the farmers live in town and commute to their fields, the way they do in some of the Asian countries?"

"Well, not exactly," she explained. "Nobody owns particular pieces of ground in the farm domes. That was tried, but it wasn't practical. Most of the people aren't farmers; agriculture's a specialized, scientific thing, particularly here. So the farm is a cooperative and homesteaders receive financial shares in it. They buy food like anybody else."

I didn't really understand it at first. How could shares in the farm be given to arriving homesteaders without decreasing the value of the original holders' shares? Later, when I studied how the Colonies are set up, I discovered that the whole thing was underwritten by the government when the life-support system and the initial domes were installed. This business of reserving shares for new homesteaders was all part of the original charter. It's complicated, but the effect is that by the time they retire, a homesteading couple will end up with outright ownership of their farm shares; they can sell them or pass them on to their children, along with their apartment, free and clear. They get the same high salaries as nonresident workers, too. The contract they sign to get free passage from Earth says they both have to hold jobs for at least ten Martian years, except while on maternity or disability leave. It also says they have to have at least two children, and may have as many more as they want tax free, because the whole idea behind subsidized fares is to build up the population.

Of course there's a lot more to New Terra than the residential domes. There's the equipment for extracting oxygen from the ground, for instance. We left the industrial domes, the power and atmosphere plants, and the waterworks for another day, but we did take a quick look at one of the farm domes. I was happy to see all those healthy-looking plants, though I knew their vigor came from chemical feeding, without any help from the Martian soil.

Before going back to the hotel, Dad and I stopped at a store we'd noticed across the mall, but buying a dress proved to be easier said than done. We hadn't known about the thirty-week minimum delay between placing an order and getting it filled. The store was expecting a few open-stock clothes in as soon as *Susie's* cargo was unpacked, but I found that there was a waiting list a mile long on which my name naturally didn't appear. The clerks were more than a little shocked that I could need something already, having just gotten off the ship; as we went out, I overheard some disparaging remarks about "tourists."

I had only one recourse: to borrow something from Janet. She was staying at the Champs-Elysées; I called her, and went over. We managed to pin up her blue microfiber shift so that it wasn't too awful on me. Janet hadn't gone in for Colonial fashions, either; she would have been the very last person to say, "When on Mars, do as the Martians do." So I can't say that I looked stylish. But after all, I thought, I wasn't a Colonial, and why should anyone expect me to dress as if I were?

Dinner that night was as miserable as I'd thought it would be. The one and only bright spot was the note of pride I heard in Dad's voice when he introduced me as, "My daughter, Melinda." I just hadn't anticipated the extent to which we were going to be welcomed into Colonial society. It wasn't until much later that I began to understand how vital it is to New Terrans to have firms like Dad's invest in Mars, and how proud they are to show off their accomplishments to anyone from the mother planet.

There's a lot less formality surrounding the governor and other officials in the Colonies than there is on Earth; we were not only welcomed, we were the guests of honor. It was a big dinner party: Governor Matsumoto and his wife, Mr. and Ms. Ortega, and at least a dozen others, all of whom went out of their way to be cordial. I sat there in my ill-fitting, pinned-together dress, with my face burning and the air seeming even more stuffy and inadequate than usual, wishing that I would pass out and not revive until I was on my way back to Earth. And the only time I managed to say anything, other than "How do you do," and "I'm pleased to meet you," it was wrong.

I was seated between the governor and a distinguished-looking gentleman whose name I hadn't caught, but who told me that he and his wife had been born in Ethiopia. There had been a long discussion about Earth's coming review of the Colonial appropriation, and everybody had agreed that it was absolutely essential that the word get back as to all that was being accomplished on Mars.

"The important thing to be put across is that this isn't just some far-out scientific experiment," said someone. "What public opinion on Earth usually doesn't recognize is that we *live* here. We're neither laboratory specimens nor a parasitic drain on Earth's economy; we're simply people fighting to be self-sufficient. What we need is the equipment to produce more of what we use—we don't want handouts."

Dad assured them that he'd help in any way he could. There was a lull, and the man on my right turned to me. "How do you like New Terra so far, Ms. Ashley?" he asked.

Well, I hadn't been paying a great deal of attention; my thoughts had been quite literally millions of miles away. And I knew I couldn't tell him the whole truth. So I answered with the first reasonably optimistic thing that popped into my head. "Oh, it isn't bad at all," I said, with all the cheerfulness I could muster. "It's so much more civilized than I expected."

There was a frigid silence. Dad glared at me, and I think he was about to say something, but Governor Matsumoto beat him to it. "We may be a frontier world," he said dryly, "but even our most biased critics have seldom accused us of being an uncivilized frontier. Times have changed since pioneers lived in rough camps, you know."

Times have indeed changed. But the pioneering spirit hasn't, and what I knew of it wouldn't have gotten me past Iowa, if I had lived in Melinda Stillwell's time.

Chapter 9

I'll always be glad that I began to understand the Colonial viewpoint a little in time to be of some help to Dad. Oh, not to share it, but at least to have some conception of what it was all about. It was because of Dad that I first tried, at any rate, for when it finally dawned on him what my true feelings were, he was terribly perturbed. He'd ignored my lack of enthusiasm on the *Susie*, thinking I was bound to get wrapped up in the excitement once I got to Mars. But after the fiasco of our first dinner party, he couldn't do that anymore.

On our way back to the hotel that night Dad came as close to blowing up at me as he ever did. We exchanged some bitter words. In his eyes I was biased, provincial, and rude, and I suppose I was. Vaguely I knew that such a bias was what Alex had been trying to warn me about, though he'd charitably assumed that I wouldn't have had it without copying Janet. Or maybe he used Janet simply as an excuse to bring up the subject. Dad was willing to make excuses for me, too; his was that he should never have left me in the same school in the same part of the world for so long. He even hinted that Gran and Maple Beach might be at the back of my narrow way of thinking. At that point, I retreated into my room and slammed the door.

But neither of us could stay mad for very long. I could see that my remark hadn't been exactly polite, and that Dad had every right to be embarrassed by it, considering the company we'd been in. And Dad admitted that I was entitled to my opinions. "Mel, honey," he said, "it's just that I want you to have the whole of life for your horizons. I don't want you earthbound—literally, or figuratively, either. You don't have to like Mars; just don't condemn it automatically, without recognizing what's happening here."

It took me a while to figure out what he meant by that, but when I did, I resolved to make an honest effort to find out "what was happening." After all, I was stuck on Mars, and would be for another five months, reckoned by Earth's calendar.

The hardest thing for me was the fact that our social life didn't stop after one evening; Dad got acquainted fast, and we were entertained several times a week. At the beginning I was sure I could never go to another dinner with those same people. But Dad insisted that I couldn't insult them again by refusing, any more than they could fail to include me in their invitations. So I went. It was the only thing I ever really did for him. I don't kid myself that I came to Mars merely for Dad's sake; there was too much else involved. Attending those dinners was different. Personally I wouldn't have cared what the leaders of Colonial society thought of me if I hadn't had to see any of them; but Dad did care, and his job was important to him.

The people we met were nice to me, but cool. Word had got

around; the antagonism wasn't all one-sided. Most Colonials are chauvinists, though their background does encompass two worlds, and the smallest slight to their city is a worse offense than any personal insult could ever be. At first, I didn't see the other side of the coin, the kind of camaraderie New Terrans have that isn't found anyplace on Earth nowadays. Sure, they're stiff-necked about their pride in the Colonies, and they bristle when you contradict that. But it's natural enough, when you stop to think what they've gone through to build this place. Their society's a tight little circle, as well-fortified as the dome itself, but you don't have to be anybody special to be accepted into it; all you have to do is treat Martians as human beings, not as if they were little green men or something.

It's funny how my worst problems on Mars were things that I hadn't anticipated in spite of all my doubts. It seems ironic that the most unpleasant aspects of those first few weeks grew out of situations that might have existed anywhere. In between the dreaded social engagements, I was bored. Just plain bored! I don't know what Dad had thought I would do on Mars while he was wrapped up in his work. There are just so many hours that you can alternate between a hotel room, the library, and the public park. Janet's entire life revolved around the biology lab; Alex was working; and I didn't know anyone else besides Dad's friends. For that matter everyone's busy on Mars, even the children. And you can't get to like a place by loafing.

The old fear still haunted me, but not so much as I had expected it would. New Terra's so big and substantial looking that it's hard to think of its having an artificial atmosphere. Occasionally, going through one of the wide-open emergency airlocks at a building's entrance, I would get the shivers thinking of why it had been built that way, though there was some comfort in the knowledge that even if the dome should be punctured there'd be plenty of time to get inside before that airlock would be sealed. (The same setup's used in the tunnels between domes, but it's not noticeable there because you go through them only in subway cars.) All the same, I had no desire to go Outside. Alex suggested it once, but I put him off; he was terribly busy then with his new job, and for a time he let it ride.

I saw Alex and his family about once a week, and it was the one thing I really looked forward to. The first time, Dad went to the Prestons' with me. It was certainly a contrast to those other dinner parties; everything was happy and relaxed and natural. Ms. Preston was a lively, warmhearted person whom I liked immediately. Young Alicia was very much like her, with the addition of some thirteen-year-old enthusiasm. Mr. Preston was calm and confident and strong, and it was easy to see whom Alex took after. Alex was—well, *Alex*. It was almost as good as seeing someone from home.

Dad took us all out to the best restaurant in the city a few days later, but since he was usually tied up with his business associates I was afraid we wouldn't see the Prestons often. Alex asked me out the very first weekend, and it was then that I told him about Ross, whom I somehow hadn't mentioned specifically before. I don't think Alex was surprised, though. The next night his mother called me and asked me to dinner again, and I decided that going to his family's, when invited by his parents, was not exactly the same as dating. When I got there, Alex treated me just like a sister, and that's how it was from then on.

It was the sort of family that I'd always wished, secretly, that I'd been born into. Not that I would have wanted to trade Dad in for Mr. Preston or for anybody else; but together the Prestons seemed to have something. Whatever it was, Mars was about the last place I'd have expected to find it. The way they lived certainly couldn't have had anything to do with it. Always before, when I'd imagined family life, I'd pictured—well, a real home: a place with a big living room, and books lining the shelves, and curtained windows looking out on a yard where the children could play, and maybe even a fireplace. And a kitchen smelling of home-cooked food, and silver tableware reflecting candlelight, and fragile, antique china dishes like Gran's for Sunday dinner. None of those things were possible in the Colonies. The Prestons' apartment was just like a thousand others on the outside, and on the inside it had the kind of modern decor I've always hated. If it could be called "decor," that is; the furniture was rather sparse. Half the time Alex, Alicia, and I lounged on the floor. They had to clean the dishes from one meal—not wash them in *water*, heaven forbid, but stick them in the sonic cleaner—before they could set the table for the next. It wasn't that the Prestons were poor; actually they were quite wealthy by Earth standards, though only in the middle brackets for New Terrans. But things just aren't available on Mars.

And still, in a way I envied them! I envied Alicia especially, which was a crazy thing. Considering she'd never even seen Earth, I'd have thought I would have been sorry for her. Only

Alicia didn't know what she was missing, and she did have parents, at an age where parents are very important. And she had Alex, permanently, for a brother.

One of the first times I went to the Prestons' they had other guests: Alex's cousin Paul Conway, the minister, and his wife, Kathy. Kathy and I hit it off right away. She was a small, auburn-haired girl who didn't look old enough to be a teacher, let alone the mother of three children; and she had a warm, easy laugh. Paul didn't seem old enough or solemn enough to be a minister, either, though actually he was in his thirties. He had been educated on Earth, as Alex had, and had met and married Kathy there.

"I grew up in Chicago," she told me. "Right in the middle of that jam-packed, smog-ridden labyrinth that's had no improvements since the twentieth century. Too many people, too much noise, and too much weather—not just cold winters, but heat and humidity and temperatures that change every day, not to mention snow and rain."

But there were easier escapes than this, I thought. "What really made you come to Mars?" I asked curiously.

She closed her hand over Paul's. "Need you ask?"

I shook my head, unconvinced. They were so obviously in love, and yet was that enough? A normal person's life was bound to Earth. If she'd been born a Martian, that was one thing; but if she hadn't, the unnatural conditions in the Colonies offered no permanence, no foundation on which to build anything enduring. A marriage had to be enduring, and weren't there some things that were more basic, more important even than love? Yet Kathy had given birth to her children on Mars. She expected to die on Mars.

"Don't kid the girl!" Paul chuckled. "Don't give her the idea that I dragged you off without giving you any say in the matter."

"Well, I didn't have to marry you."

Alex said, "I think Mel really wants an answer, Kathy. Do you have any reasons of your own for being here, or are you just putting up with it for Paul's sake?"

"Of course I have reasons. This is an exciting place to be. And there are three very personal ones—Charlene, Teddy, and Ellen."

"You left out Paul Junior and Tim. And who in the world are those last two?"

"The ones we haven't had yet. Seriously, Paul and I could have had our first two sons on Earth. We could never have managed the excess population tax for more, nor would we have felt it was right to increase Earth's population. That's one reason we feel that what we're doing to develop the Colonies is important, important for the human race, I mean."

"You mean because Earth is overcrowded?" I asked. "But from that standpoint, what difference does it make whether you have children here, or you stay on Earth and don't have them? If Mars is populated by people who wouldn't have been born on Earth anyway, how does that help Earth's problem?"

Alex said, "The number of people on Mars hasn't anything to do with it, Mel. It's a well-known fact that Earth's population increases much faster than people can emigrate to Mars, in spite of all that's been done to control the birth rate. Even if we had twice as many ships that would be true. But it's not the point."

"The point is that here on Mars we're learning how to colonize a new planet," Paul said. "The technology, the know-how, is being developed."

"So that someday, when Earth is really out of room, other worlds can be colonized, too," Kathy added.

"Yes. Because someday—not in our time, but *someday*—the human race will be in great danger if it can't expand. Many of us believe that that danger can be averted if we start learning what we have to know before it's too late." Paul continued.

"I don't understand," I said. "There aren't any other planets that we could ever colonize. Venus is too hot and the outer planets are too cold, and they all have such dense, poisonous atmospheres that even domes wouldn't be any protection."

"Right," said Alex. "There aren't any other planets, not in our solar system."

I stared at him. "You mean—the stars?" I demanded. "Seriously?"

"It's a very serious matter."

"But look, Alex, I wasn't much on science in school, but even I know that it's not considered feasible to go to the stars. Not ever."

He laughed. "You also know enough about history to know that there was a time when it wasn't considered feasible to go to the moon."

Paul interrupted, "When they first did go to the moon, many

people wondered why. They questioned whether it was worth all the money and effort spent on it. The same thing was true of Mars. And many people still think that the money appropriated for the Colonies could be better spent to raise the standard of living on Earth."

I flushed, unwilling to confess that I'd always thought pretty much along those lines myself. I wanted to find out what Paul was driving at.

"I believe that's a shortsighted view of things," he went on. "I believe that we're morally obligated to have as much concern for future generations as for our own."

Kathy said, "It's like parents choosing to raise their own standard of living rather than to provide for the future of their kids. You wouldn't consider that very admirable, would you?"

"No—but I still don't see how colonizing Mars is helping. I don't see how we know that it will ever enable us to colonize planets of other stars." I looked down at my plate, deep in thought. Where was the line between the real and the fanciful? Some things were hard to believe, but still true: that we could be sitting in an ordinary-looking room on the planet Mars, eating synthetic chicken off blue-rimmed plates, for instance. Yet other things . . . Interstellar travel? Surely, in stories! But *seriously*?

"We don't *know*," said Paul. "I have faith that it will, because colonization is the only truly long-range hope I can see for humanity. There isn't any other answer. The day will come when Earth cannot support its population. Maybe they'll resort to compulsory control, enforced by methods that would destroy every vestige of individual choice—"

"Or maybe," Kathy said, "there'll be a war that will kill off half the people and set civilization back thousands of years."

"I refuse to believe that there has to be a choice between those alternatives," Paul told me. "I think the need for it can be prevented if we start in time. But we've got to proceed step by step. Mars is one of those steps."

"The key to interstellar expansion's not going to be handed to us when it's so late in the game that the average man in the street can see that we need it," Alex said. "Not without any preparation."

"I suppose not," I agreed doubtfully. Put that way, it sounded important enough. But oh, dear—it was very idealistic and all that, but it wasn't the whole answer. Not for an individual person, that is. Kathy didn't act as if she were making a noble sacrifice for the sake of future generations; she acted as if she *liked* Mars. As if she was comfortable in New Terra, and happy to stay. And everybody I met felt the same way.

I'll have to admit that all the people on Mars seem to be—well, nice. Of course, it's the most selective society that has ever existed, because of all the screening that goes on before immigrants are accepted. (Selective in a good way, I mean. Naturally the people are of all races and nationalities and come from all kinds of backgrounds, but none of them are criminals or moochers or anything.) All the people are fairly smart, too; they'd have to be to hold the kinds of jobs that are available. But more than that, there isn't any sort of snobbishness among New Terrans.

It's a curious fact, but most Martians have more money than

they know what to do with. They may have been penniless when they arrived; lots of homesteaders are. But Colonial pay has to be high to attract nonresidents to temporary jobs, since there aren't enough homesteaders with the skills necessary to cover all the essential ones. Also, practically all the permanent settlers have either earned or inherited homestead rights on top of their salaries. Although prices are high, there's hardly anything to buy; and luxuries aren't available at any price, even through private import, because so much space on the ships has to be given over to priority shipments. And with the twenty-kilo baggage limit enforced the way it is, everybody starts even as far as possessions are concerned.

When I first began to understand this, it seemed awfully frustrating. What good was mere money if you couldn't use it? "It's so pointless," I protested to Alex. "Giving up all the things money's good for, just to accumulate it. Even homestead rights don't amount to any more than that."

Alex was shocked. "You're confused, Mel. Nobody cares about the money, accumulating it, that is. It's doing something with it that's important. If you have more than you need to live on you can afford to invest in things with long-term benefits. There's a lot we can manufacture from Martian minerals once we can afford to bring in the equipment. That's got to wait till we have more people, but someday—why, we'll be able to export, and have more ships so we can import more things. We'll be self-sufficient eventually; we won't need any subsidy from Earth at all. And we'll have independent government, too."

Well, this was a subject dear to Alex's heart, and I soon

learned not to get him started on it unless we had at least an hour to spare. Colonial self-sufficiency, that's the big dream! New cities, gleaming like the alabaster ones in the old song, cleaner than Earth's and without poverty. Local industries, new jobs— unlimited opportunity for everybody. New Terra's only the beginning; there'll be other cities, and all sorts of exciting challenges to come.

"Do you really think it's practical?" I inquired meekly once. "I mean, in such an artificial environment. Being so dependent on power for air and water and all."

"All cities are artificial environments, even on Earth. Some of them have been since way back in the twentieth century. What do you think would happen if the power went out in a place like New York or Los Angeles? Or if the water system failed?"

"I don't want to think about it."

"They'd be in just as bad a way as New Terra would, I can tell you that. That dome up there doesn't make us dependent, Mel; modern civilization does. It's true everywhere, only here you can see it."

"I'd rather not see it, thank you. I'm a country girl at heart."

"If we don't start building cities off Earth, the time will come when Earth has no country left. What then?"

What indeed? The same unanswerable argument. We always seemed to get back to that.

Of course, Alex didn't really think that everything on Mars was perfect; he was too much of a realist for that. "I get carried away," he confessed. "It's not going to be as grand as I make it sound, I suppose. But we dream. That's what pioneers have always done, isn't it?"

"Maybe it is," I admitted.

"You should know," he said with a grin. "You with your romantic ideas about your pioneer ancestors."

"Oh, Alex, that's not the same thing."

"Isn't it?"

"They weren't trying to develop a technology or anything. They lived off the land; it was a good land, and that's why they settled it. They didn't have to fight it, make it into something that it wasn't."

"You mean it's still just the same as it was before they arrived?"

"Don't try to confuse the issue!" I sputtered. "You know what I mean."

"Yes, but do you? Why do you like history, Mel?"

"Well, I—I guess because life used to be so much simpler in the old days, so much more understandable."

"Yet history's the story of change."

"That's a depressing way to look at it."

"Why? I think it's exciting. And you're wrong about things being more understandable in the past; they weren't, not to the people that lived then. It's only true looking back."

"The pioneers who came to Oregon didn't have the kind of problems you do on Mars!"

"No. They had their own. Disease, starvation, fighting with the native Indians—and by the way, at least you've got to admit we aren't taking land on Mars from people the way Americans took land from the Indians, which makes our kind of pioneering quite an improvement."

We got into discussions like this often, not only about Mars, but about other subjects: the news from Earth, movies we'd seen—all sorts of topics. It was stimulating. Ross never discussed anything with me, and he wasn't interested in the whys of things. I'd hardly noticed until I began to get his letters. They were dull, really; he never seemed to have much to say. I told myself that Ross wasn't particularly good at expressing his feelings in words and that it wasn't fair to judge him by them. I read the letters over, trying to picture just what we had done on our dates, and it was surprisingly hard to remember. Ross had been *there*, that's all. And when we were in love, what difference did something like talking together make? What Alex and I had was friendship, which seemed another thing entirely.

The days dragged along. Dad got more enthusiastic about the Colonies all the time. He was finding not only that it would be good for his firm to have a Martian branch, but also that the firm's investment would be beneficial to Mars, and that made him very happy. As he got busier, the social whirl subsided a bit, much to my relief. I still hated formal parties, although I had more or less inured myself to them except for gatherings that included a Madame Lin, who had not yet forgiven me for my no-longer-expressed Terrestrial provincialism. Ms. Ortega had become almost a friend; she was really a kind, motherly person, and I felt less uncomfortable at her dinners than at the others.

On my birthday Dad gave a dinner in my honor in one of the hotel banquet rooms. (It was sweet of him, and I did my best to enjoy it; I couldn't help thinking, however, how much nicer it would have been to be with Ross—or with Alex.) Also, somehow he got me a new dress, a lovely gold one. I still don't know how he managed it. I had been borrowing frequently from Janet and from Kathy, and he realized that it's awfully frustrating for a girl to be the official hostess for her father when she hasn't any suitable clothes.

I went to church each Sunday, not only because I wanted to hear what Paul's sermons would be like (he was very dignified in the pulpit, almost a stranger) and because I knew Alex would be there, but even more because it was a link with home. The same hymns, the same ritual, so many millions of miles away! I could imagine Gran back at Maple Beach hearing those same lovely words. It wasn't the denomination I'd been brought up in, and naturally the church itself didn't look a bit like any I'd seen before, though I had to admit that inspiring effects could be obtained with low-gravity architecture. But some things, I guess, are universal. Whatever had made me think that a human settlement on Mars would be alien?

Alex and I got into the habit of going home after church either with his parents or with Paul and Kathy Conway and spending all afternoon and evening there. Occasionally Dad joined us, though his work kept him well occupied even on weekends. I didn't see Alex on weekdays, and I didn't know whether he was dating anyone or not; if he was, he never mentioned her. Most of his friends seemed to be young married couples, but then all the homesteaders are married, and even the second-generation Colonials tend to marry young.

When I saw how Kathy had fixed up her living room, I stopped thinking that a person can't be individualistic in an apartment. She hadn't had much more to work with than Ms. Preston, though she had managed to bring a few personal doo-dads from Earth, but the effect was entirely different. Not better, exactly, but unique. For instance, Paul and Kathy's place boasted a window. Not a real one, of course, but a mural draped to look real. As to where Kathy had acquired such a huge painting— well, not being an artist herself, she'd projected a color slide on the wall and filled it in from that. It just goes to show what imagination can do. The most striking thing about Kathy's window, though, and the thing that made it believable, was that she hadn't chosen a scene from Earth the way I probably would have. It was a Martian landscape, with red hillocks and all; and it wasn't half so desolate looking as I'd have thought it would be.

The Conways' home was always a lively place because of the kids: Paul Junior and Tim, who were five and four, respectively, and little Charlene, who was not quite three. It surprised me that Kathy was so cheerfully nonchalant about them. Those kids meant more than anything in the world to her, but she never seemed to worry! She even sent them out to play by themselves, and since there was no yard, that meant the public park.

I asked her about it once. "But there's really nothing that could happen to them, you know," Kathy said. "Not here. Now if I had to keep track of a child in a place like Chicago or L.A., where there's traffic to contend with, or contagious diseases, not to mention whatever unsavory characters might be wandering around the streets—"

The boys were old enough to know about Earth, and they had a thousand questions about it.

"Billy Johnson says on Earth you can get a glass of water without paying for it," Paul Junior announced. "He says you can even splash in water. That isn't true, is it?"

"Of course it's true."

"Can you get free Cokes, too?"

"No, you have to pay for Cokes." Hadn't Kathy ever told them? I wondered. It was a while before it occurred to me that if she had, they might not have distinguished her stories about Earth from the ones she'd told them about Peter Rabbit or the Three Bears.

"Maybe I'm going to Earth someday," Paul Junior told me. "When I'm big."

"*I* wouldn't want to go to Earth," Tim broke in. "It's too far away."

How sad, I thought, for it to be so far away! I'd always wanted children, wanted to give them love and warmth and security and faith in humanity's traditions. *Earth's* traditions. It was another matter to bring them into a hostile, artificial world, a world where they'd be trapped inside a sealed dome under which they could never draw a breath of unfiltered air, and where they'd be exposed to countless dangers, yet would know few if any of the natural experiences of growing up.

Alex didn't look at it that way. Kathy didn't. "What's 'natural,' except what you're used to?" she once said to me.

All right. It was a good theory, and I was convinced that it was fine for the Prestons, the Conways, for Dad even. But for me—that was another story. I did my level best to work up some of the same spirit that the others had; but I was still homesick on Mars, and the pull of Maple Beach was as strong in me as ever.

Why did it seem to matter, since I was leaving in a few months? I didn't know. I only knew that it bothered me. I should have felt happy each time I saw a new date on my handheld computer's calendar, knowing that the time was coming when I'd be safely back to Earth, to free air . . . and Ross. But I wasn't; neither was I at all ready to admit that my feeling might have anything to do with Alex.

Chapter 10

In spite of the fact that I was getting used to Mars, I still couldn't bring myself to go Outside. Dad went a couple of times with people he knew, but I refused. I knew that it was cowardice, plain and simple—there's no nicer word for it—yet it was a thing I just couldn't face. And it was silly. Of course stories are told about groundcars getting stuck in the sand or otherwise stranded and running out of air, but that's not very frequent; not frequent enough to keep New Terrans from going, or from taking their kids. On Earth stories are told about cars breaking down in the desert and the occupants dying of thirst, but people drive in the desert anyway, with sensible precautions. There's no difference, really.

It was the "running out of air" idea that scared me.

And after all, why should I go? It wasn't as if there were any real need to. Alex tried to convince me that there was. "You can't go back to Earth without having seen any of this planet!" he insisted.

"I've seen it from the monorail, coming in from the spaceport. I'll see it again on the way back."

"That's not enough to count. I don't understand you, Mel.

Here you're always complaining about us being 'sealed in' under the dome, yet you won't leave the dome when you've got the chance."

"I can't help how I feel about it," I said miserably. "I just don't happen to be as fond of living dangerously as you are."

"Living dangerously? Kathy took Paul Junior and Tim Outside three months ago!"

"I thought you told me once you were ten before you first went?"

"I did, and I seem to remember your saying you couldn't understand why I hadn't insisted on going before. It was more of an event then, because groundcars were harder to come by."

"Well, nobody needs to make an effort to get hold of one on my account."

Alex shook his head. "Mel, sometimes I think you're not fond of *living* at all," he said, almost angrily. "All right, there is a risk attached to it. Nobody can promise you that you're going to be one hundred percent safe Outside, or here in the dome, or anywhere else for that matter. It's just the way things are, and if you're going to crawl back into your shell every time that fact occurs to you—"

"Do we have to talk about it?"

"No, of course we don't," he said, softening. "Keep your illusions, if they make you happy. Only—"

Only they weren't making me happy, I realized. And he *cared*. That was why he said these things; it was as if he were really my brother, and he cared. But it wasn't going to do any good. I was the way I was, and I'd be glad when I was back at Maple Beach, where the risks were familiar things that I could cope with.

In the back of my mind, though, was a trace of a suspicion that even at Maple Beach things might not be just the same as before. That shell, maybe, was already cracked.

One Sunday when we had been in New Terra for about four weeks, Kathy and I got to talking about teaching. I planned to teach high school and she taught third grade, but she told me that there's a lot of common ground. Kathy had a huge class of fifty eight-year-olds, but she had a teacher's aide to help her, one of the young homesteader brides who was still in college. (There aren't nearly enough trained teachers in the Colonies.) "I wish I could do something like that," I said. "It's just deadly sitting around the hotel, and I can't spend all my time in the library."

"It must be," Kathy agreed. "Why don't you enroll in the university, Mel?"

"But I won't be here long enough."

"Yes you will, for one term. A new one starts next week, and it will only last a month and a half."

"A month and a half? Oh, you mean Martian months. Twelve weeks." It was a thought, all right. It just hadn't occurred to me that it would be possible. "Will they take me without any transcripts or anything?"

"I don't see why not, as a special student. They're not very formal about things like that, with so many homesteaders coming from all kinds of schools all over Earth. Why don't you go and see? If you can do it, you'll have advanced standing when you get home."

Paul agreed that I probably wouldn't have any trouble getting accepted and interrupted his chess game with Alex long enough to dig out a course catalog he had stashed away somewhere. I pored over it while Kathy put the kids to bed. When the game was finished, Alex came and looked over my shoulder.

"American history, English, French . . . are you kidding, Mel?"

"What's wrong? Those are normal freshman subjects, aren't they? I thought I might as well get them out of the way."

"Do you really want to know what I think?"

"Yes, of course."

"Well then, I say why waste your time? Why not take subjects that you won't get the same slant on anywhere else?"

"Like what, for instance?"

He took the pad and pencil from me and wrote, *Colonial History, Biology, Descriptive Astronomy*—and, after a slight pause—*Introduction to Philosophy.*

"Oh, Alex, I haven't any background in those things!"

"I know."

"But that's an awfully hard schedule—"

"I thought you had time on your hands that you wanted to fill up." Kathy started to say something, but Alex shushed her. "Look, Mel," he went on, "you don't think you'd flunk any of those courses, do you?"

I said heatedly, "No, certainly not! I've never flunked anything."

"Then give them a try. For one thing, survey courses here will cover stuff that isn't touched at the undergraduate level on Earth outside of specialized courses that you wouldn't have time to take. For another, there'll be no grades to worry about; they don't give anything but 'pass,' 'fail,' and 'honors.' "

Doubtfully I agreed, "I guess it would be silly not to take advantage of the chance, then, as long as I'm here." I knew I was committed. It was bad enough being timid about things I had no aptitude for; I wouldn't want him to think I was afraid of college work, too.

The next morning I went over to the campus, which is in East Dome, and talked to the registrar. "Sixteen units?" he said, making it sound ominous.

"Ycs, isn't that all right?"

"I suppose so, since you're a special student and you're not working." He stamped my cards with only a trace of visible reluctance.

From that time on, I didn't have the problem of boredom anymore! It was a real strain to keep up; even Sunday afternoons had to be given over to study. When I was with Alex he tried to help me, but that wasn't always too successful; Alex had a way of getting off onto something perfectly fascinating that had nothing whatsoever to do with the next day's assignment. Janet helped me, too, with my biology course, one time when I went over to return another borrowed dress. My social life with Dad's friends was being sharply curtailed, since I had to study evenings, and I can't say that was a disappointment. My presence was not really required, for the obligatory round of formal affairs was over and, increasingly, the talk centered on business.

The University of Mars isn't set up like American colleges. There's no fooling around, and no busy work. There are lectures (by some of the top people in their fields, incidentally), but outside of that you're on your own. You don't have to work through specific lessons at a computer terminal except for required quizzes that have due dates. You don't have to study at all, as far as that goes; nobody checks up. But if you don't pass that final exam, well, you don't, that's all. You repeat the course until you do. I knew I wouldn't be able to repeat any courses, and I was bound and determined to show Alex that I could pass them. Toward the end I was working day and night, practically, in my room with my handheld computer after library hours. Dad kidded me, but underneath he was proud of my ambition, and from what he said I gathered that his friends had commented on it, too.

It was surprising how fast those twelve weeks went.

When the term ended and I got my course certificates—with no "honors" but no "fails," either—Alex insisted on taking me out to dinner to celebrate. (Paul and Kathy went, too, so it wasn't actually a date.) We went to the Star Tower, which is the only place in New Terra from which you can really see the sky. It's a tiny dome between two of the big ones, reached by subway like everything else, and it's crystal clear instead of translucent, as the regular domes are. The lower level is a restaurant and the upper level's a terrace for stargazing; the two are joined by several open, winding staircases that are very light and airy looking, like all low-g construction. On most nights there's dance music after twenty-one o'clock, but we went early.

"Now it can be told," Alex announced cheerfully, over dessert. "One term hour at the University of Mars equals a unit and a half at any American university. You're going to get twenty-four credits when you transfer."

"Oh—!" I sputtered. "Alex Preston, I don't know why I put up with you!" Then, noticing the look on Kathy's face, I accused her, "You must have known, too, all along."

"We told Alex it was a dirty trick," she admitted. "But he had some convincing arguments."

"Which did you enjoy most," Paul asked me, "your first four weeks here or the last twelve?"

Well, they were right, of course; it had been just what I needed. I hadn't had time to notice whether I was on Earth or on Mars or on the twelfth moon of Jupiter! And moreover I *had* learned a lot, all kinds of things that I'd never even thought of before. It's funny how much exists that you're just not aware of even when you think you've got your ideas all neatly organized.

The second Friday after the college term was over happened to be Christmas. It wasn't anywhere near December 25 by the Martian calendar; it was August 41, as a matter of fact. But Colonial Christians celebrate Christmas whenever it comes on Earth, for otherwise it would fall at 668-day intervals because of the greater length of the Martian year.

Christmas without a tree. Christmas without chimneys, or holly wreaths, or strings of colored lights. Having spent few Christmases in cold climates, I didn't miss snow. But Christmas without shopping! That was the strangest thought of all.

No, not quite the strangest. Because somehow I'd always thought of Christmas as an *Earth* holiday. "Peace on Earth," after all . . . and yet I guess "Goodwill to Men" applies anywhere. I guess all the really important things apply.

We were to spend the day with the Prestons, all of us—Paul and Kathy and the kids, Dad and I. Luckily, I was forewarned about the presents; Paul Junior said something that tipped me off. The gift-giving custom hasn't been abandoned in the Colonies, it means even more, I think, because people have so little in the way of things. The lack of goods in the stores means that the status gift and the business-obligation gift are simply not around, but to people you care about you do give, and it has to be either something you can make or something of your own.

When I first caught on, I was unhappy because I had nothing to give anyone. But then I realized that I did have: the handknit sweater I'd brought! It would serve a purpose on Mars after all. I unraveled it carefully and, swallowing my reluctance, I borrowed some lightweight knitting needles from one of Ms. Ortega's friends, who'd been unaware that as a New Terran she'd have no use for them. Then in the weeks before Christmas I knitted frantically whenever I wasn't studying. Not that anybody would need heavy socks on Mars, but it was soft, lovely dark blue stuff, real wool, which none of them except maybe Kathy and Alex's parents had ever possessed. I knew that even the kids would be delighted.

I ran out of yarn before I could make anything for Dad, but he'd often admired the little wrist camera that Ross had once given me; surely Ross would understand, and Dad wouldn't object to its being slightly used looking. As I wrapped it in colored foil saved from a lunch container, I thought of how different this Christmas was from the one we'd spent together last year, in Washington. Then, if someone had told me that my next holiday season would be spent on Mars, I'd have thought it was a joke. You can never see what's coming, I suppose; and with some things, it's very lucky that you can't.

Christmas was a day that I'll always remember as my first truly happy one in New Terra. I don't suppose the light beaming down through the dome was really any different than it was on any other day, but it seemed to sparkle, somehow. We came out of church with the lilt of the carols still singing in us and walked all the way to the Prestons' with a bright buoyance that had nothing to do with the low gravity. *O tidings of comfort and joy, comfort and joy, O tidings of comfort and joy!* I marveled at the sudden knowledge that there was the same amount of comfort and joy on Mars as anywhere else.

Paul and Kathy stayed at church to greet people as they left, and by the time they got to the Prestons', Alex's mother and I had dinner on the table. It wasn't very fancy fare; though I was well used to synthetic meats by that time, no one can claim they're the equivalent of roast turkey. But dessert was special, a real fruitcake, brought back from Earth by Alex (half a kilo out of his twenty!). "Extravagant," he admitted, "but it's something Mom always said she missed."

After dinner we gathered around in an informal circle on the living room floor and lit the candle. A candle is a very magical thing on Mars because it has to be imported at great expense and delay; the shops do stock a few at holiday time, but a person has to be in line by five in the morning to get one. There is something about an open flame, though, that just can't be duplicated. The thin Martian atmosphere won't support fire, but naturally the air in the domes will—only there's no wood. That single candle was the closest thing to a blazing hearth that Alicia and the children had ever seen; in fact, the closest that Alex had seen before he went to Earth. I wouldn't have thought it would have seemed very impressive to me after all the wintry nights I'd spent in front of the big stone fireplace at Maple Beach. And yet it did. I can't explain it, except maybe to say that there's a unique aura to Christmas candles wherever they happen to be found.

While our candle burned we opened the presents. There were thrilled gasps from Paul Junior, Tim, and Charlene, though they didn't have nearly as many packages as children usually do and they didn't have any illusions about Santa Claus. Even the adults found something exciting in exchanging gifts, something that's lacking, maybe, when all people do beforehand is to load up at a shopping mall.

The Conways gave me dress material, which I later learned Kathy had ordered for herself almost two years before and had only just received. From the Prestons there was a fabric-lined box to keep my beads in, as well as homemade candy; they had some for everyone, and I know it took a good share of their sugar ration. My gift from Dad I'd received earlier that morning: a small portrait of Mother that he'd carried in his wallet for many years.

Alex's gift was another book, well-worn and with underlining, since it was one of his favorites. (There are few actual books on Mars; normally people go to the library and download the electronic version.) "I hope this is a more suitable choice than the last one," he told me, smiling. It was. It was Robert Frost's poems. When I got back to Earth, I vowed to myself, I'd send him a new copy no matter how much the shipping charges were!

Later that evening, when the candle had burned down to the last blob of wax and all the presents had been admired and ahhed over and put carefully aside, we decided to go to the Star Tower. Everyone went, even the children; a look at the stars was a rare treat for them. We walked all the way across the dome along the Champs-Elysées before going down into the subway, just because it seemed like a nice thing to do. It was odd not to have the air crisp and cool, though, on Christmas night.

"I have a suggestion for those fabulous new cities of yours," I told Alex. "Turn the thermostat down once in a while! Seventy-two may be 'ideal,' but it's tiresome."

"It might be a good idea," he agreed, "if we had warmer clothes. Not that I'll ever have anything to say about it."

"You will have," Alicia bantered. "When you're a city councilor or a governor or something."

He turned fiery red. "Come on now, Alicia—"

It was the first time it occurred to me that Alex might have political ambitions, but when I stopped to consider it, I knew that it would be perfectly natural if he did have. Much as he might want to run his own business, it was quite obvious that he had the ability to go beyond that eventually; for Mars really was going to have new cities, and it would be people like Alex, who'd put their hearts and souls into the Colonies, who were going to be the leaders. Standoffish as I was with those I'd met through Dad, I could see that politics wasn't the same kind of game in New Terra as it usually is on Earth. Governor Matsumoto, for instance, wasn't a "politician" in the sense I'd always thought of one; he was the sort of man that people just naturally look up to. Like Alex would be, grown twenty or thirty years older.

The Star Tower was crowded; a lot of people had had the same idea we'd had. The place was full of noise and laughter and the exhilarating ring of recorded Christmas music. We didn't take a table but went right upstairs to the dome. It was unlighted except for a glow around the circumference, and above, spattered across blackness, were the stars.

I leaned back against Alex's shoulder and craned my neck to stare upward. We saw them as they were never seen through Earth's atmosphere, or in the *Susie*, either, when she was under spin. White and pure and unblinking, they shone like a thousand Christmas Stars at once. There was one that was much bigger and brighter than the others, though; a disk more than a point.

"What's that?" I asked. "Alex, I think it's moved since I've been watching!"

"That's Phobos."

"The little moon, you mean—the one that goes around Mars in only seven hours or so?"

"Yes. Say, that's another thing you ought to do, Mel—go to Phobos. I'll have to see what I can arrange."

"Don't you dare!" I protested, laughing. I was beginning to be wary of Alex's ideas about what might be good for me to do. "Can we see Earth?" I asked, to change the subject.

"No, not now, it's too close to the horizon. It's an evening star or a morning one, you know, because it's closer to the sun than we are."

I gazed out at the glittering arc of the Milky Way. All those suns, less widely spaced near the center of the galaxy, and lots of them with planets—according to Alex, according to Paul, even, planets where humans will someday walk. Below in the restaurant, caroling had replaced the recorded music. "Hark! the herald angels sing, glory to the newborn King!" The volume increased as the singers came up the stairs. "Born to raise the sons of earth, born to give them second birth. . . ." *The sons of Earth*, I thought. *Even now, more than two thousand years and fifty million miles away from Bethlehem, we are all the sons and daughters of Earth. We always will be, no matter how far from it we go.*

Alex reached for my hand and for a moment gripped it tight. "Mel—"

"Yes, Alex?"

"I—well, I—"

I turned to see his face, then quickly pulled my hand away and stepped back. He was not looking at me as if I were Alicia now.

"I'm sorry, Melinda," Alex said. "It's nothing. No, maybe there is something. Look, are you getting married just as soon as you get back to Earth?"

"Married?" Somehow I hadn't thought much about it recently. "Yes, I guess so. Sometime during the summer, anyway."

"That's definite?"

"Yes, it's what Ross and I have planned ever since our junior year." *And I must tell Dad,* I resolved. Why hadn't I told Dad during all the time we'd been together? He wouldn't object, he'd be happy for me; and he must have guessed anyway, since I wouldn't date anyone else.

"Well, look," Alex persisted, "if you were ever to change your mind or anything, you'd let me know, wouldn't you?"

"Let you know? But Alex, I'll only be here another three weeks." *Three more Sundays,* I thought suddenly. "I'm not going to change my mind before that. That is, I'm not ever going to change it—oh, you know what I'm trying to say!"

"I know," he said softly. "It's just that, well, I hope I'll hear from you to know you've made it safely back to Maple Beach and all, and—and I wouldn't want to send you a wedding present if you weren't getting married."

Three more Sundays. Of course I could hardly wait to get back home, and yet it was impossible to believe that after three more Sundays I would never see the Prestons or the Conways again. I would never see Alex again. What would it be like to look at this red planet from my window at Maple Beach, and imagine all of them still living on it?

Those three weeks went even faster than the three before my final exams, I think. I was nearing the end. There was no need to be homesick so near the end. I could even relax a little, the way

Alex was always telling me to, and not bother to worry over any-thing. And maybe that's why I gave in at the very last minute and went Outside.

Dad and I were going home on the *Susan Constant*, which had made a round trip while we had been on Mars, although several other ships had arrived during our stay. And, by the same alphabetical scheme that had put us on the first trip down when we arrived, we were assigned to go up on the first sched-uled shuttle.

It takes more than a day to load a departing liner because Mars has only a few shuttles. That means that the first people to board have to leave a day early, and we were going on a Saturday morning. A few days before, during our last dinner at the Pres-tons, Alex said to me casually, "It's a pity you aren't going to be here Saturday, Mel. Alicia has to go Outside to finish a school project, and I promised to take her. It would be the ideal oppor-tunity for you."

"Ideal from whose point of view?" I said lightly, though I knew perfectly well what he meant.

"Mel," Alex insisted, "you'll be sorry when you get home. Your friends will ask you what Mars looks like, and you won't be able to tell them."

"That's not why you want me to go."

"Maybe it isn't. But it will be fun, Mel. Remember how I had to talk you into trying zero-g, that first week on *Susie*?"

I did remember, and I remembered that he had been right. I also remembered that if he went Outside on Saturday morning, he wouldn't be able to see us off at the spaceport. And surely nothing could happen to me on my last day! Feeling very reckless, I said, "All right. If we can change our shuttle reservations, I'll go with you." That put it nicely into the hands of fate, I thought.

Changing our shuttle reservations proved to be easier said than done, however; lots of people had reasons for wanting an extra few hours on Mars. There was only one seat left on a flight late enough to do me any good. Dad said, "Take it, Mel. I'll keep to the original plan and meet you on board *Susie*."

Early Saturday morning, after we checked out of the hotel, I kissed him good-bye at the monorail station on my way to the airlock to meet Alex and Alicia. We stood talking for a few minutes, waiting for the train to arrive. "When is the firm going to open its office here?" I asked him.

"In a year or so. These things take time to arrange, but I've done all the groundwork. There's no question about its being both feasible and desirable. That's what I've said in my final report, the one I transmitted yesterday."

"Dad—do you want to head up that office?" I finally came right out with the thing that had loomed in my mind for some time as a distinct possibility.

"It's not a question of my wanting to. They will choose someone younger, Mel. You can't turn back time, and my time for pioneering is long gone." He smiled at me. "It's not a thing to feel sad about, honey. I've been offered a vice presidency! And when it comes to Mars, I can contribute more back on Earth just by my influence."

The train was ready to board. Though we were only going to

be separated for a few hours, I hugged him tight. Just before he stepped into the car, Dad turned back to me. "Has it been as big a thrill for you as it has been for me? Mel, honey, have you enjoyed being on Mars?"

I knew what he wanted me to say. "Of course I have, Dad," I told him. "I'm awfully glad I came."

The last, at least, was true.

Chapter 11

The seasons aren't noticeable in New Terra, but Mars has them: spring, when the frost of the polar cap melts, sending rivulets of moisture down the arid rills; summer, when the usual drought returns, and dust storms often haze the otherwise cloudless sky; fall, which is summer only more so; and winter, which is similar but colder. Not that even summer is warm, but in winter the temperature is always far, far below freezing.

The day we went Outside was a glorious late summer one, without a dust cloud in sight. People can walk around on the surface of Mars in pressure suits, but I drew the line there! We went out in a pressurized groundcar that was rented by the hour. There is a complicated ritual for checking equipment and emergency supplies; Alex went through it matter-of-factly with the airlock attendant while I tried not to watch. Then we got in and Alex checked the seals on the car door while the attendant closed the inner door of the lock. Soon a low, nerve-jarring whine started; they were pumping the air out. I pressed my lips together, sorry that I wasn't on the shuttle with Dad.

"Relax," Alex told me firmly. "You're holding your breath! You aren't going to feel anything." And we didn't; when the lock pressure was low enough, the outer door simply opened, and we drove out onto a well-worn track in the red sand.

Alicia's school project involved photographing the city from the outside for a classroom display. She thought it a fine assignment; they had literally drawn them out of a hat and most of the class was stuck with things that could be done inside the domes. I was merely thankful that she hadn't drawn rock collecting, for which we would have had to use suits.

We headed in the direction of a ridge a little way off where Alex thought we would get a good view. There was no danger of getting lost, since we would never be out of sight of the domes, but we had to stay in radio contact anyway; it's a requirement that groundcars be tuned in to the Ground Control frequency at all times.

"Think of all that virgin territory out there," Alex said, pointing off in the distance. "Most of it's never been seen, let alone driven through."

"Never seen!" I asked. "After all the years the Colony's been here?"

"The part within range of these groundcars has been covered fairly thoroughly," he told me. "But since the atmosphere won't support aircraft, there's no way to go any farther except in one of the shuttles, and that's an awkward business. A shuttle can only make spot landings, and it can't be gone when there's a ship in port."

"The terrain's been photographed from orbit, though," Alicia said.

"Yes, and from the research station on Phobos, but that's not the same thing as surface exploration. Mars has about the same land area as Earth, allowing for Earth's oceans, and it will take a long time to explore it all."

He swung the car around so that we would get a good close-up of the domes and stopped. "There, Alicia. Try it from here." She knelt on the seat and pressed her camera close to the window to snap the first shot.

"Can I download a copy to keep before I leave, Alicia?" I asked.

"Sure, Mel."

"I want one, too." Alex said. "But I want to take my own." She nodded and handed the camera over to him. But it wasn't at the view that Alex pointed it, nor was it at his sister. I might have fixed my hair better, if I had known beforehand.

"I love this!" Alicia exclaimed as we started to drive again. She added wistfully, "I wish today could go on and on forever."

"So do I," Alex muttered, not taking his eyes from the bumpy terrain ahead of us.

"Do you like it Outside as much as all that?" I asked him.

"That wasn't what I was thinking of."

"Oh," I said unhappily. Endings were always hard, I thought. I shouldn't have come; I should have known it would only draw it out.

Alicia teased, "You better watch out, Mel. Alex would like it if we got stuck out here, and you missed the ship."

"I wish it were as simple as that." He threw me a grin. "You trust me, don't you, Mel?"

"Probably I shouldn't," I said good-naturedly, "but I do."

"I was right again, wasn't I? Being out here isn't so bad?"

I had to admit that it wasn't. It's funny—with some people, if they're always right, it only makes you resentful. You begin to wish they'd be wrong once in a while! But with Alex I never felt that way, except on rare occasions when we were both mad. He was right, but he wasn't trying to prove anything by it. The warm circle of his confidence spread out to include me, and it was a thing to depend on, not to resist. He made me feel confident, too.

Out there in the sunlight nothing seemed very frightening, and my nervousness was almost gone. From our vantage point the city was breathtakingly beautiful, rising out of the richly colored ground as it did, and there was a certain thrill in being afloat in the Martian wilderness that was more pleasant than I had expected. It would have been a pity not to have come; it's true enough that you miss a lot by setting limits for yourself.

Especially since whatever bounds you set don't really make you secure.

We were called back before the morning was half over. The controller wouldn't tell us anything over the radio; he made it sound like a routine order, as if he needed the car for a priority job or something. When Ground Control tells you to do a thing, you do it, so Alex turned back immediately.

"It's too bad, though," he complained. "Just when you were starting to enjoy yourself." Alicia was loudly indignant, though she had enough pictures. I sat silent; inexplicably, the dread of disaster was returning.

When we got into the airlock, we could see through its inner window that another man was waiting with the lock attendant;

as soon as the pressure equalized and we got the doors open, he came forward. It was Paul.

I knew something was wrong just from his voice—it was his minister's voice, not that of the friend I'd laughed and joked with so often. He took my arm and led me into the crowded little Ground Control office. "Melinda," Paul said, "I don't know any way to tell you this except directly. There's been an accident. . . ."

There are some things you can never be safe against, no matter how well you plan your life. Change is one of them; how young I was when I thought I could live forever at Maple Beach, and never change! Fear is another. And still another is grief.

The *Susan Constant* wasn't hit by a meteor; she was hit by the shuttle during an abortive rendezvous attempt. The people killed didn't die from lack of air. Their death was no worse than any death in a collision, and I've been assured that it was instantaneous. The accident wasn't even unique to space; what happened was just plain equipment malfunction, of the sort that has occurred countless times on Earth since humans first began to have equipment.

It could have been much, much worse. That first shuttle carried more supplies than passengers, and *Susie* herself had only a skeleton crew aboard. All in all, less than twenty people were killed out of the two hundred or more who might have been involved. That was little consolation to me, though, since one of those people was Dad.

There was absolutely nothing anybody could have done about it. As Janet once told me, rather too triumphantly I thought, "it was bound to happen sooner or later." But not because space is a particularly dangerous place; only because life *is* dangerous. There have always been accidents, and there always will be. They are rarer now than they once were, but the possibility is always there, on Earth or on Mars or anywhere. Knowing that is part of living.

This philosophic view of it wasn't my first reaction, of course. It's something that Paul couldn't get across to me until a great deal later. That first day all I could think of was that once, the very last day on Mars, I'd denied my fears long enough to go Outside with Alex—and look what had happened! I'd been sure that something awful would occur if I went, and it had.

"Don't say that!" Alex told me insistently. "That's completely irrational. It's backward, even; your dad didn't change his shuttle reservation, you did. If you hadn't come Outside with us, you would have been killed, too."

That was true enough, but it wasn't exactly a comforting thought.

To the Colonies, while the death of twenty people was a terrible tragedy, the loss of *Susie* and of the shuttle was a matter of even more serious concern. The full implications of this didn't hit me until the following day, when I had cried all I could for the time being, and the sedative Alex's mother had given me had finally forced me into more than twelve hours of exhausted sleep.

The previous day had not been my last one on Mars. My last day on Mars had retreated somewhere into the dim, unpredictable future. The *Susie* was not going to Earth and there were almost two hundred people like myself who would be competing for places on the sister ships that would be arriving at rarer-than-normal intervals. Yet compared with the problem of outbound shipping, our plight was not very significant. New Terra, already short of supplies, was going to be still shorter.

The Preston family was discussing this at the lunch table when I dragged myself out of bed to join them. (I'd stayed with them overnight; only when I woke up did I realize that I had been given Alicia's bed and that she had spread some blankets on the floor.) "It's hard to believe," Ms. Preston was saying. "The *Susan Constant* was an institution. I guess we all expected she'd last as long as the city."

"I can't bear it," Alicia said tearfully. "Poor *Susie*—she was such a nice old ship, and it wasn't her fault! I never got to go aboard her. Now I'll never go to Earth in her—" Seeing me, she broke off. Alex scowled at his sister and got up to stand beside me.

Alicia apologized rapidly. "Mel, I'm sorry! I didn't think—that is, I didn't mean—"

I tried to smile. Because I really couldn't blame Alicia; I knew that if that sort of feeling hadn't been overshadowed by my sorrow for Dad, I might have grieved for *Susie*, too.

"I hope you don't think we're all being sentimental over a ship at a time like this," Mr. Preston said to me. "Our chief concern is for those men and women, naturally. All the same, the destruction of the ships themselves is a real blow because of what it's going to mean here. You realize, don't you, Mel, that they can't be replaced very soon?"

I nodded, not trusting myself to speak calmly. A spaceship is just not a thing for which a spare can be kept in reserve. A liner like the *Susan Constant* costs billions, and can't be built overnight in any case. Even replacement of the shuttle would be a major proposition, and a shuttle couldn't travel at *Susie*'s speed; if a new one started out from Earth right away it wouldn't arrive for more than a year, the current positions of the two planets being unfavorable. Doing without that shuttle was going to be hard on the Colonies, not only because loading and unloading of the remaining liners and freighters would be slowed down, but because exploration of Mars itself would have to be cut back.

Slowly, I took in the fact that I might be stuck on Mars for a long time. Most of the other ships were freighters that used slow, economical orbits or that carried only those passengers authorized by government priority. And though departing liners were normally less crowded than arriving ones, Mr. Preston warned me that there was talk of temporarily converting most of the cabin space on incoming ships to cargo space, to make up for the urgently needed supplies *Susie* would have carried. If that happened, the ship probably wouldn't be converted back for the return trips. For one thing, there wouldn't be the crew or facilities aboard. An extra passenger could be taken on in an emergency, of course, but I wasn't an emergency case; my personal feelings didn't constitute any sort of crisis, except to me.

Dad . . . and now Maple Beach, and Ross, beyond my reach. When the only thing in the world I wanted was to be back there. Gran. If only I could talk to Gran! Or walk on the beach, as I always did when there was an unhappy fact to be faced. At the beach house, the winter surf would be crashing on the sand below and the gulls screeching overhead, and the blue-papered west bedroom would be dark and empty, the lovely old quilt neatly folded across the foot of the mahogany bed. . . .

That afternoon, Alex and I walked along the West Mall away from the Etoile, between the too-neat beds of marigolds and Shasta daisies and other terrestrial flowers, looking up through the dome at the shut-out sky and talking. "Oh, Alex," I said, "*why*? Why did it have to happen?"

"You don't expect me to give you an answer."

"No," I admitted. "I guess I don't."

"Maybe Paul could make a try at it, I don't know." He stopped, and turned to face me. "I do know this much, Melinda. It wasn't because you came to Mars. You mustn't ever think that it was."

"But if we hadn't come, Dad wouldn't have been on that shuttle. Oh, I wish spaceships had never been invented!"

"That's like saying that if firearms hadn't been invented no one would ever have been shot. True, maybe, but meaningless, because who's to say what else would have happened?"

"I suppose you're right."

"It's not easy to be objective about a thing like this," he went on, "but all the same you've got to try. Ever since the conquest of space began there have been occasional disasters; yet we can't give up space travel because of that, any more than people abolished automobiles because of the traffic deaths, or stopped using coal because men were trapped in the mines sometimes."

"I know."

"Some people will say that we should, especially with all this debate over the Colonial appropriation going on right now. There are going to be some emotional appeals in the Terrestrial press. They won't be pleasant reading, Mel. You'll have to remember that if that kind of thinking's followed through to its logical conclusion, we might as well all live out our lives in our own homes without ever venturing out of the front door. And even there we wouldn't be safe; I seem to remember reading that one of the first men to orbit Earth was injured by a fall in his own bathtub. Lord, I know it's hard to accept! But if you're completely honest with yourself and think of your dad, you know that's what he'd tell you."

I couldn't argue. That was exactly what Dad would say; I couldn't even imagine his saying anything else.

"Don't be sorry you came, Mel," Alex pleaded. "Your dad wouldn't want you to be. I know he wouldn't. He told me once how happy he was to have had the chance to come, because seeing Mars had been a dream of his for such a long time. Don't be sorry he got the thing he wanted."

"My mother wanted to come to Mars, too," I said slowly. "She couldn't, because of her heart, but maybe if she'd come sooner—before it was so bad—she wouldn't have died from it at all. It's true that there's less heart disease here because of the low gravity, isn't it?"

"Yes, it is. They'd be sending heart patients to hospitals here, or anyway to Luna City, if there were a way around the high-g liftoff."

"In any case," I told Alex, "I'm not sorry I came with Dad. If I hadn't, we would never have been together at all." I began to cry again. "Alex, I was never close to him! Not close the way your family is. I wanted to be, but I just couldn't. He was more like a friend than a father."

"Maybe that was better than the other way around. I've seen a lot of kids who weren't friends with their parents, who won't have the good memories of their dads that you have." He pressed my hand. "I know that's not going to help. I—I don't know what to say, Mel."

Reluctantly I drew my hand away and started walking again, swiftly this time. "Don't try," I said as he caught up with me. "Don't try; there isn't anything anyone can say."

The public memorial service for the people who had been killed was held in the City Auditorium, and was conducted by the leaders of New Terra's six major religions. The music was beautiful, the eulogies inspiring, and I sat through it dry-eyed. I didn't feel any emotion at all. It was unlike most Colonial funerals in that there was no need for a closed-circuit TV hookup to the cemetery, which is located Outside within a nearby circle of low hills. There's been a monument erected there since, though, with all the names.

I was much more affected by the private service that Paul held. What surprised me was the number of people there: not just the Preston family, but Dad's business associates and a lot of the church members. None of them could have felt any obligation, for they'd all been at the official memorial service. But they came. The Ethiopian couple, Mr. and Ms. Ortega—even Madame Lin, who I'd been sure was so cool to me. Many of them came up to me afterward and asked if there was anything they could do.

"Why are they acting like this?" I whispered to Kathy. "It's just the same as it would be at Maple Beach. Yet I'm not one of them. They all know what I think about Mars."

"For heaven's sake, Mel," Kathy replied, "when will you understand that Earth or Mars has nothing to do with it? They liked and respected your father, and they sympathize with you. Isn't that enough?"

In spite of everyone's sympathy, however, I felt very much alone. Gran wrote to me, of course, and that was some help; but there isn't any real answer to sorrow, other than the one that time brings.

My most immediate problem was finding a place to live. There was no chance of getting back into the Hilton, and the Champs-Elysées was full, too. Nor could I go on staying with the Prestons; even if they had been able to get hold of another bed, there would have been no place to put it in Alicia's tiny room. I finally decided that the best thing for the time being was to go to Janet's, since her room happened to have a convertible sofa. Janet was scheduled to leave on the *Oregon Trail*, which was due in another ten weeks, and I'd then have to make other arrangements; but I would cross that bridge when I came to it.

"I hate to impose on you like this," I told her. "First I borrow your clothes, and then move in on you—"

"It's perfectly all right," she assured me. "We Terrestrials have got to stick together. You don't know how glad I'll be to have your company, Mel. I've been awfully lonely."

The first night at Janet's, while she was off at an evening lab session, I wrote a long letter to Ross. I was feeling sorry for myself, I guess; anyway, I poured out all my longing to be back on Earth as well as all my grief. And I said something else, I'm not quite sure why. "It's not fair," I wrote, "to expect you to go on indefinitely without dating. Ross, darling, I want you to know that I won't mind if you go out with other girls before I get back. I'm afraid we are going to have to put off our wedding for a terribly long time."

Mail travels fast between planets, much faster than ships. When the relative positions of Earth and Mars are favorable it takes only a day or two, even allowing for the long queues, and transit to the relay stations when the planets aren't in line doesn't add much time. Before the week was out I got back a message that I didn't know quite what to make of.

I had gone a little overboard, maybe, in the things I had said to Ross about the fix I was in. But, naturally, I hadn't expected him to do anything about it. After I'd sent the letter off, it had occurred to me that there might possibly be an element of "I told you so" in his reply. However, I wasn't at all prepared for what happened.

"Dear Mel," Ross had written. "Don't worry, I'm not about to do any dating without you. You're my girl; you always will be. Darling, I am terribly sorry about your dad, but thankful that you were not on that shuttle, too. How did it happen that you weren't? Luck must be watching out for you, and I'm going to do all I can to help it along. I'll see to it that you get back to Earth where you belong without any more delay, so don't worry on that score, either. Got to rush now—I'll let you know just as soon as I can."

This was certainly a hopeful-sounding note, and I couldn't see why I felt disturbed over it. Ross was assuring me that he wouldn't think of dating anyone else; surely, I thought, the thing I felt when I first read that couldn't have been disappointment! Had I, underneath, wanted an excuse to see Alex on less of a brother-sister basis?

But my uneasy feeling seemed stronger than that. What had Ross meant, that he'd see that I got back to Earth without any delay? How wonderful if he could! I told myself that perhaps I was just afraid to get my hopes up, for I really didn't see how Ross could help at all. Why, he himself had once mentioned how hard it was to get reservations on a spaceliner. Suddenly I remembered the exact words he'd used. *It takes pull to get a place on one of those ships on short notice. My father had to fix it up for somebody once. . . .*

The next time I saw Alex, I asked him, "How would a person go about getting a ticket on a spaceship without being put on the waiting list?"

"I'm afraid there's not a chance in the world, Mel. I thought we explained that to you." He hesitated. "You realize, don't you, that the fact that Dad and I work for TPC doesn't mean we have any power to—"

"Oh, I know there's nothing you can do in my case. I was just wondering. I've heard that it sometimes happens, that's all. From the Earth end, I mean."

"Well, then I guess you've also heard that money talks."

"I suppose if someone had a ticket he wasn't going to use, he could sell it for more than the regular fare. But I should think that that would be a pretty rare case."

"It is. What's more, it's illegal. That wasn't what I was thinking of, though. There are some other ways that don't depend so much on chance."

"I don't see—"

"Mel, wherever there's a government priority list for anything, there's a way to get on that list. Usually there's a way to get placed at the top of it. It's in the same class as fixing tickets, buying votes, and cheating on the income tax; some people don't see anything wrong in it."

"Oh," I said in a low voice. "I've been just—naive, I guess." Very naive, maybe. I had often heard that Ross's father had "connections" in various branches of the government; I'd assumed this meant merely that he was a successful attorney, and had met a lot of people. I had never stopped to think what might be implicit in the words "pull" and "fix it up."

Of course I didn't *know* anything, really. But I began to dread the next letter from Ross.

Chapter 12

The weeks after Dad's death were bad ones. Besides my grief, the longing to get back to Earth got worse and worse, until sometimes it seemed as if I couldn't stay in the Colonies another minute. When I'd had a reason for being in New Terra and a definite departure date to look forward to, it had been one thing; but since my stay was no longer purposeful, Mars was like prison. (I'm surprised that airless planets aren't used for penal colonies; they would be a lot more escape-proof than Devil's Island ever was! There wouldn't even be any need for guards.) Yet what bothered me most was the thought that I might be offered an avenue of escape all too soon. A chance I couldn't take advantage of was going to be a lot worse than no chance at all.

And there was another problem. Being with Alex wasn't a help anymore. It made me aware that I might not be as content at Maple Beach as I'd always expected to be. Having a plan for your life is all very well, and even when it's disrupted temporarily you can hang on tight and see it through. But once you begin to suspect that you might care about things that don't fit into that plan, or into any plan that you'd ever want . . . Alex had tried to teach me what I'd been missing out on, and he'd done too good a job of it.

I was alone too much. I was welcomed at the Prestons' and at the Conways'; I had occasional invitations, too, from some of the older people Dad and I had known. Everyone was very kind. But that only filled weekends and a few evenings, for I couldn't get back into college until the start of the next term. It was the same old problem again: Everyone who didn't go to school had a job. I began to wish that I was skilled in something so that I could work, too, although I wasn't short of money because Dad's firm was continuing my expense account for as long as I was stranded. There are no jobs in New Terra for people without training, though; anything that doesn't require an expert is either automated or eliminated because of the personnel shortage.

In the evenings, there was always Janet to fall back on. And I'd have been better off if there hadn't been. Janet's letter to the editor of *Interplanetary Observer* didn't have anything to do with me, really, except that Alex and I got into a fight over it. Still . . .

Considering how I've always liked to think things through, it's odd that I didn't do it the night Janet showed me the letter. Sometimes you can think too much, for too long, I guess, so that when you really ought to, you're tired. I was weary enough, certainly; in those days I was just dragging myself around half the time. I couldn't imagine why, since I never did anything very tiring, and usually people don't get as tired under low gravity.

I had known all along what Janet's beliefs about Mars were, and I had honestly thought I agreed with her. I'd said so often enough. So there wasn't anything surprising in her showing the letter to me and expecting me to be delighted with it. There wasn't anything surprising in her writing a letter to the editor, either, Janet being the kind who liked to make her opinions known. *Interplanetary Observer* publishes a whole page of such letters every week.

I was in bed when Janet came in that night, but I had the light on and was writing a letter to Gran. Janet switched on the coffeemaker, then came over and sat on the arm of the open sofa bed, passing me her handheld computer after bringing up a file she'd evidently stored earlier. I looked sadly at her, thinking how she was everything I was wishing to be—assured, smartly dressed and beautifully made up, brimming with energy and confidence. "Read this, Mel," she said, sounding pleased with herself. "Tell me what you think."

I was half-asleep. It was a long letter, and difficult to digest in the dazed state I was in. Janet had written:

> Having spent many weeks on the planet Mars, I believe that I am qualified to say that there is no possible justification for the ill-advised attempt that is being made to establish a permanent colony here. It is doomed from the outset, for conditions on this worthless world are such that terrestrial life can never establish a real foothold. It has, in fact, been known since the nineteenth century that the environment of Mars is irredeemably hostile. To say that humans can adapt to it is no more logical than to

say that they can adapt to a perpetual existence in outer space. Survive for a limited time, maybe; but adapt, never!

Meanwhile, uncounted billions are being squandered on this senseless project, and innocent people are being duped into tossing away their lives for it. There was a disaster here not long ago in which a whole shipload of people died horribly, for nothing. But the cost in human misery is not limited to such needless calamities. The inconveniences of living in this mechanical maze of synthetics are absolutely incredible. The willingness of people to put up with them, on any basis other than that of a short-term scientific expedition, is testimony to the persistence of human folly.

This folly might be condoned if it served a worthwhile cause. But the majority of the people here are not concerned with the advancement of science at all. They are homesteaders, lured by the promise of free land. This promise is a myth. There is no free land that is worth anything. These helpless pawns are thus forced into a parody of living that offers them far less than the normal life from which they were so foolishly attempting to escape. True, residents here claim to have "political freedom" and "financial security." What good are these, when they will never provide any of the material benefits that make living worthwhile; when despite an excess of paper wealth, few if any of these people will ever be rich enough to buy a ticket back to the only planet that will ever offer anything of true value to human beings? Let's put a stop to this nonsense, and start channeling some of these misspent funds into scientific research of a less ill-founded nature. . . .

It went on and on like that. "Well, is it clear?" Janet demanded. "Could I make it any stronger, do you think?"

"I think it's very strong indeed," I said, overwhelmed. "It's—impressive. A little *too* strong, maybe."

"You don't sound very enthusiastic." Obviously, she was hurt. I hesitated, not knowing what to say. Taken individually, none of Janet's statements were actually untrue. Those that were not facts were mere expressions of opinion, not outright lies. Why then did the total effect seem so questionable? The letter was persuasive, certainly, and yet. . . .

"What's the matter?" she persisted. "You agree with it, don't you?"

"Janet, I—I don't know."

"Aren't these the same things I've said to you any number of times? Haven't you said them yourself?"

Had I? Not quite in those terms, I didn't think. Not lately, anyway. . . . "Are you really going to transmit this?" I asked, handing the little computer back to her.

"Of course. Somebody's got to speak out." She frowned. "I

know what's bothering you," she said briskly. "The part about the accident. Mel, maybe it seems heartless of me to put it that way, but believe me, it has to be done. You've got to face up to harsh reality! You want to do everything you can to prevent the same thing from happening again, don't you?"

"Yes, certainly I do, only—" There was a flaw somewhere, but I was too worn out to analyze it. "I don't want to talk about it, Janet," I said. "I'm going to bed." I reached over and shut off the light.

Interplanetary Observer, like many Terrestrial magazines, is transmitted to Mars by data link and posted to the local Net minus the advertising, which wouldn't pay very well in the Colonies. New Terrans gladly pay for current reading material; they're always hungry for more of it. When a new issue comes out it's read within hours, letters to the editor and all. This time was no exception.

Alex read that week's *Interplanetary Observer* on a Sunday afternoon when he and I were at the Conways'. Paul and Kathy were over at the church at some kind of meeting, and we were staying with the kids. Paul Junior and Tim were in their room playing space pirates and I was getting Charlene down for her nap. Alex was paging rapidly through it on his handheld computer—he reads at a prodigious rate—when suddenly he let out a yell that I could have heard from Outside. In fact he used some expressions that ordinarily weren't in his vocabulary.

"For Pete's sake, what's the matter?" I called to him.

"Mel, come in here!" he shouted at me.

I lifted Charlene into her crib and went back to the living room. Alex scowled at me. "Mel, have you read this thing?"

"What thing?" I asked innocently, though I had a pretty good idea. I hadn't known what issue it would be in, or even if they would publish it; privately, I had hoped they wouldn't.

"You know very well 'what thing.' Did you see this before it was sent, Mel?"

"Well, Janet did say something—"

"Did you see it?"

"Yes," I admitted. "I saw it. But I didn't read it through very carefully."

"Do you mean to tell me," he demanded angrily, "that you knew that a thing like this had been written, and you did nothing to stop it?"

"There wasn't anything I could do about it, Alex," I protested. "It was Janet's idea; she wrote it, and she sent it in. It didn't have anything to do with me at all."

"She's your roommate, isn't she? You could have talked her out of it. You could have—" Suddenly he broke off, staring at me as if I were a stranger. "Or do you agree with Janet?" he asked slowly. "Does this represent your opinion, too?"

"Not exactly. Oh, Alex, you know I don't look at everything just the way you do. I wouldn't express myself the way Janet did—"

"I hope not!"

"But she is entitled to her opinion, after all."

"You haven't answered my question."

I took the computer from his hands and read the letter

through, line by line. It seemed worse than it had the night I'd first seen it, somehow. Then I had been sleepy, but now I was wide awake. Phrases like "no possible justification," "duped into tossing away their lives," and "persistence of human folly" jumped out at me in a way that they hadn't before. Finally I told him, "I don't go along with most of Janet's conclusions. But some of these things are facts that can't be denied. A little exaggerated, maybe, but—well, it's just how she interprets them."

"Distorts them, you mean. Mel, don't you realize that you or I could sit down and create an equally bad case for anything—the voyage of Columbus, the Plymouth colony, the first trip to the moon, or anything—just by playing around with half truths and emotionally charged words that way?"

"Maybe so. But Janet's got the right to free speech, the same as anyone else has."

"Legally, yes," he agreed. "But this isn't honest, reasoned dissent, Mel. It's a very skillful job, one that uses every trick in the book to arouse readers on an emotional level and confuse them with facts that have no relation to the issue. Not subtle enough for some purposes, maybe. She overplays it. But for the average voter it should do quite nicely, I think. Do you want to see a replacement for *Susie* built, or don't you?"

"Do you really think a thing like this could make a difference?" I asked. Somehow I hadn't thought of Janet's letter as having any particular consequences. And actually I don't think Janet did, either; she was just resentful because she hadn't wanted to come to Mars, and that colored her thinking.

"If you mean do I think one letter will swing the balance, probably not," he admitted. "There will be plenty of others to counter it; I may write one myself. But public opinion's not a thing to play games with, Mel. Stop and think about how many people read *Interplanetary Observer,* people who don't know anything about the Colonies at all."

Janet had signed herself as "Dr. J. Crane," I noticed. Technically she was entitled to; she did have a Ph.D. in biology. But to some people those two little letters before her name would make her an authority.

Alex pulled me around, making me look straight at him. "You've heard us talking about how critical this whole business of the new appropriation for the Colonies is ever since you arrived here—since back on the *Susie,* even," he said. "You heard your own dad talk about it, and you knew what was in the report he was sending back. Yet you didn't even try to stop Janet. You didn't take any stand against this at all."

"I—I just didn't think of it that way, I guess."

He let go of my shoulders. "I'll never figure you out, Mel," he sighed. "I know you don't think much of Mars as a place to live for yourself—no one expects you to. Not everyone's a pioneer at heart. But I thought by now you understood how the rest of us feel well enough to grant us the chance to have a go at it."

"But I do!"

"Did you tell Janet that? Did you make any effort to get her to see both sides?" Grabbing his computer back, he began to scan the letter. "Listen to this: 'a parody of living'—is that really what

we've got here? 'Helpless pawns'—anywhere but in this magazine, that would be funny! 'Material benefits that make living
worthwhile'—is that what makes it worthwhile for *you?*"

I thought back. New Terran Christmas, a parody? People like
Kathy, helpless pawns?

Janet began with an insinuation that spending time on Mars
would in itself "qualify" not only herself, but anyone, to make
these assertions. I had spent as much time in the Colonies as she
had. Were they also my assertions, by default?

"Mel," Alex insisted. "How could you possibly read a state-
ment like 'a whole shipload of people died horribly, for nothing'
without challenging it? Is that—"

"Oh, please don't!"

"Is that your reaction to being hurt—to strike out, without
caring what you strike at?"

"That's not fair!"

"If it's what you really believe, I feel sorry for you. Or are you
too wrapped up in your own little dream world to believe anything at all?"

I turned my back on him. "I don't know, Alex," I said dully. "I
don't know what I believe anymore."

"Are you afraid to find out?"

Maybe so, I thought. *Oh, Alex—why do we always argue about
Janet when it's not about Janet at all? And why do you always have to
be right?* But what I said was, "It isn't really any of your business
whether I am or not."

"Perhaps it isn't," Alex said. "But Mel, I've got to think either
that you do agree underneath with the substance of this, or that

you don't agree and yet wouldn't speak out." Still angry, but with sadness, too, he added, "Either way, I guess maybe we don't have as much in common as I thought we did."

That night I dreamed that I was in a boat, back at Maple Beach, only it was a peculiarly shaped boat and there were no oars. Also there was a gaping hole in the bottom. By all rights I should have been drowned, but you know how dreams are; the hole didn't seem to matter, except that it scared me. The tide, surprisingly, was going in and out at the same time—don't ask me how it looked, because I can't describe it, I just *knew* it was. Far away in the distance I could see the shore, and the house, and the big old fir tree wrapped in fog, and wisps of smoke rising from the stone chimney. But out to sea was a tall-masted ship, and I could hear more voices coming from there than from the land; but they were all receding.

In the morning a letter from Ross came. With shaky fingers I downloaded it, hoping that my suspicions would prove to be silly—but knowing better. Ross said nothing direct, but his words left no possible doubt, either. I don't know whether he thought I was idiotically innocent or so "sophisticated" that I wouldn't object. I'm not sure which would be worse.

"Darling," the message said. "It's all arranged. Within a few days you'll get official notification that you've been given priority passage on the fast freighter *Ares*, which is due into Mars about three weeks from now. By the end of May you'll be home, and we can go right ahead with the wedding as we originally planned. Mom is already starting to make preparations; I assume that's all right with you? We don't have to wait much longer. . . ." At the end there was a postscript: "By the way, this is costing a lot, but my dad's willing to advance it. After all, you'll have plenty once your father's estate is settled."

As I read it, I began to feel a little sick to my stomach. It hadn't occurred to me before, but Dad had been doing well and was probably heavily insured, besides which he had been traveling for the firm, which must have had a lot of accident coverage. It was true enough that I could now be considered something of an heiress. Ross's assumption about how I'd choose to spend part of Dad's money was bad enough, but beyond that—had he thought about the money before he'd decided to "go right ahead with the wedding"?

I could believe it. It was awful to know how easily I could believe it! It didn't really matter whether it was true or not, because if the idea wasn't a shock to me, it wasn't possible that I could be very much in love with Ross. And somehow that wasn't exactly a shock, either.

I knew, of course, what I had to do. In a case like that there's no question; the thing that looks like a choice isn't a real one. You make all the choices beforehand by being who you are, and the painful part is opening your eyes to the thing you *can't* choose. That, and the worrying before the time comes.

It was a hard letter to write. Not because my heart was broken or anything like that, for actually it wasn't, but because I didn't want Ross to think that the problem was just my not being willing to go along with his shady dealings. I wanted him to understand very clearly not only that I wouldn't be on the *Ares*, but that this was the last letter he was going to get from me, regardless of what ship I went home on. All in all, I must have written about a dozen drafts, but before that day was over I drew a deep breath and sent the thing off, extra-charge rush transmission, so that it would be sure to reach Ross before any money changed hands.

It was a relief. It was the biggest relief I'd ever felt in my life, but I wasn't very lighthearted over it.

I was free now, free to date Alex. Only now there wasn't much chance that he would want to. And that was probably a good thing because there couldn't be any future for us; Alex's life was bound to Mars just as surely as mine was bound to Earth, and there was nothing that either one of us could do about it.

Alex would go on believing in the Colonies and working for them and someday he would become "a city councilor or a governor or something" as Alicia had predicted. I wasn't cut out for that sort of life and I couldn't be anything but a hindrance to him, even if I wanted to stay, which of course I didn't. Sooner or later my name would come up on the waiting list for passage back to Earth, and I would go home to Maple Beach to live with Gran. I would finish college—though not at the university where Ross was—and then I would be busy with my teaching career. I'd have the lifestyle that was right for me. Very probably, I decided, I would never choose to marry anyone.

Part Four
PHOBOS

Chapter 13

They had the right idea when they named the moons of Mars! Of course, back in the nineteenth century when they did it, all the newly found heavenly bodies were being named for mythological characters, and nobody thought of them as places to visit. When they called Mars's two little natural satellites *Phobos* (Fear) and *Deimos* (Terror), they were thinking of the horses that drew the chariot of the god of war, not of how someone would feel if he were planning a trip to one of them. But it worked out very appropriately as far as I was concerned.

I'm a great one for getting roped into things. I'd been terribly afraid of space since Janet's hysteria on board the *Susie*, and then after Dad . . . well, I knew that kind of accident wouldn't happen twice in a row, but still . . .

I never went Outside during the weeks following Dad's death, partly because I associated it with that sad morning but even more because my fear was worse than ever. As far as spaceships went, though I was longing for a place on one in order to get back to Earth, I was expecting the trip itself to be something of an ordeal. Yet off I went on a trip to Phobos, an airless planet, wearing a pressure suit, no less!

It was Paul who talked me into going, but I wouldn't be surprised to know that Alex put him up to it. In fact I'm pretty sure he did. But I'm getting ahead of myself; quite a bit happened before the Phobos trip.

A few days after Alex and I had the fight about the *Interplanetary Observer* letter, I moved out of Janet's apartment and in with the Conways. That was Paul's idea—I had gone to him for help in finding another place to live—and I didn't give him any argument, for I was anxious to get away from Janet. The atmosphere was strained between us because I had finally done what I should have done in the first place: I'd told her exactly what I thought of some of her statements.

I knew I had to, once I thought through the things Alex had said. I put it off as long as I could, but eventually I cornered her and went through those irrelevancies and exaggerations point by point. She heard me out, but after that we were just stiffly polite to each other. She knew, naturally, who I'd been influenced by, and she had her own ideas as to how and why. Janet never had much patience with people who let other people's opinions disturb them, and it was inconceivable to her that I might have had a sincere change of heart.

I didn't see Janet again after I moved. I assume she went home on the *Oregon Trail* as scheduled. Poor Janet—I don't suppose her colleagues at the biology lab were very cordial after the letter was published. It was hardly a shining example of scientific objectivity, after all. I feel sorry for her, in a way; it's funny how people who think they don't have emotions are the very ones who get trapped by them.

Things began to brighten up after I got to the Conways'. I couldn't have had dearer friends than Paul and Kathy. The kids became just like family, too; especially Charlene, who was a perfect doll. Sleeping on a cot in her room, I soon began thinking of her as my own little sister.

Friday night of my first week there, Alex came over. I hadn't heard from him since the day of our fight, but I'd known he would have to come sooner or later, if only to see the Conways. I was setting the table when he arrived; Kathy was in the kitchen, but Paul wasn't home yet. We hadn't been expecting Alex that night, and when I opened the door my first feeling was a sort of joyous tingle that was different from anything I'd ever felt with Ross. But then I remembered, *It's hopeless.*

Alex sat down on the couch and I sat stiffly on the edge of the chair opposite him. We, who had been so close, were now like strangers. Then suddenly Alex broke into his old grin and I could feel the chill disperse. "I was sort of rough on you, Mel," he said, sounding chagrined. "I get worked up about things like that; maybe you've noticed."

"I've noticed," I told him, smiling.

"Well, I just took it out on you, I guess."

"It didn't do any harm, Alex. It woke me up, I guess. I—I had a talk with Janet afterward."

"I know. Paul told me. Look, Mel, if you really agree with any of what Janet said—well, you mustn't let yourself be talked out of it, by me or anyone else. We're all prejudiced here. It's possible that we're wrong."

"Paul told me the same thing. But you're not wrong, because

it's working for you. I know that with my mind. Yet I can't seem to feel it."

"You don't have to. Why should you have any loyalty to New Terra? You're not New Terran, Mel. That's the thing I just couldn't grasp."

I didn't say anything for a moment; I just sat staring at the now-familiar landscape of Kathy's "window." Then I said hesitantly, "Alex, you asked me to tell you if I ever changed my mind—about getting married, I mean."

He leaned forward and from the way his eyes lit up I knew that he'd been serious about wanting to know. How foolish I was to say anything, I thought, to start something that couldn't be finished. It wasn't fair to *him*.

But it was too late to back out of it. Keeping my voice light I told him, "Well, it's all off. Ross and I don't write to each other anymore."

"Mel, I'm sorry." He didn't sound sorry, though. "I hope it wasn't anything—"

"Would you believe a number-one priority cabin on the *Ares*?"

"So that's why you asked, that time." Feelingly, he added, "That's too bad. I know how hard it must have been to turn down."

"Hard? Are you suggesting I had to think twice?"

He flushed. "I guess I'd better apologize again. That wasn't meant as a backhanded compliment."

"Perhaps I deserved it. Because of course there was more to it than that." I didn't go into details.

Alex stood up and paced over to the other side of the room,

then came to stand beside my chair. "Mel," he said, "how important is going back to Earth to you, now that your wedding's off?"

I made the only reply I could. "It's very important, Alex."

"I thought so," he said levelly. "I just had to be sure, that's all." Laughing a little awkwardly, he took my arm in the brotherly way that had been his habit for so long. "Come on, let's see if we can give Kathy a hand with dinner."

I had planned to take on another heavy load of college work as soon as the next term started, but before that something better happened—Kathy got me a job as a teacher's aide when one of the regular people went on maternity leave. My duties were simple enough to learn; all I had to do was to follow the teacher's directions. I supervised study groups, play periods, and sometimes the lunch room, besides handling all sorts of clerical details. The most fascinating part was the contact with the kids, though. I wouldn't have believed how interested I could get in a bunch of nine-year-olds who were having trouble with social studies because they just couldn't picture Earth. Although I wasn't authorized to conduct any classwork I did get in on a lot of discussion periods, and I found myself hard put to keep up with all the questions. How could I describe an ocean to someone who'd never seen more water in one place than he could hold in a bowl? How could I tell him what a forest smelled like, or what it was to see green blades of grass spring up from a rain-soaked field? Of course we had videos, but I'd seen videos of Mars, too, before I came; it's not the same. History was a fantasy to those kids, separated from their own world by concept as well as by time. For instance, when, in talking about American history, I described the first Thanksgiving to them, somebody wanted to know how the Indians had managed to stay alive before the first ships came!

At the beginning of the new term I did go back to college part-time, but I kept my job, too. I requested to be transferred to an older class, however, since I knew that would be better preparation for high school teaching. I was assigned to the eighth grade, with Alicia Preston as one of the pupils. My new charges were more knowledgeable than the little ones—though it was a bit disconcerting to have a thirteen-year-old boy ask me if I'd ever seen a real dog—and in things Martian they were considerably wiser than I was. Right away I learned that to New Terran children there is only one thing worthy of note about the eighth grade: the field trip to Phobos.

I vaguely remembered that Alex had once told me that like all second-generation Colonials, he had been to Phobos when he was twelve for his first zero-g experience. I was not prepared, though, for the way the thing's talked about, dreamed about, and lived for from the first grade on up. It outshines all other milestones put together, and as a long-anticipated goal is roughly comparable, I suppose, to a Terrestrial youngster's first driver's license. That's not surprising, considering how rarely these kids get Outside at all.

Phobos is not at all what I would have thought of as a moon. It's nothing but an airless hunk of jagged rock, only ten miles in diameter. The most notable thing about it is that it's got an aw-fully close, fast orbit for a natural satellite; it's less than four thousand miles out and circles Mars in under eight hours, which means that it rises in the west and sets in the east three times a day. That may sound spectacular but it isn't, because Phobos isn't very big or very bright, and you're not out where you can watch it, anyway.

But to a child growing up in New Terra, Phobos is a shining promise. Earth is full of wonders that adults seem to believe in but that are hard to distinguish from the admittedly exaggerated tales of Oz or never-never land. Earth offers more than Phobos, but it offers it on a very problematic basis. Phobos is accessible. Not continually accessible; shuttles are not launched for joyriding. But once, in the eighth grade, the chance to visit it comes. This makes the eighth grade an easy class to handle, since exclusion from the Phobos trip is just about the most effective threat that can be used on a young Martian.

Nobody *has* to go. But I never met a child who didn't want to, any more than I met one on Earth who didn't want to go to the African Game Preserve. And that was the big difference between a native Martian and me—I couldn't bear the idea! I didn't want to go at all for a long list of reasons, not the least of which was the need to wear a pressure suit and air tank. And I didn't intend to do it, either. It wasn't part of my job; although chaperones would accompany the kids, they would be volunteers from the staffs of the various schools as well as from the families of the pupils.

Naturally, Alex thought I ought to volunteer. He had done so himself, nominally because of Alicia, but I knew well enough what was in his mind. Kathy was on the committee for making the arrangements, and undoubtedly there was a conspiracy be-tween them. The kids were to be broken into groups with two chaperones, a man and a woman, assigned to each; it was im-possible for everyone to go at once since New Terra was short a ship. Phobos has a small research station to which a shuttle de-livers supplies at regular intervals, and the kids were to go along on the milk run.

"But why?" I demanded of Alex, about the tenth time he worked it into a conversation. "Why do you care so much about my doing this one particular thing?"

"Because it's an opportunity that won't come again in just this way."

"I can't see what's so urgent about my taking advantage of it." I had a sudden thought. "Is it anything to do with—with getting back on a horse after you've been thrown?"

He hesitated. "Partly. That's not the main thing, though. Mel, I've got a reason, but I'm not going to explain it right now. Can't you just take my word that it's important?"

"I'm sorry, Alex. I really don't want to go, that's all." Hur-riedly I changed the subject, and we didn't speak of it again.

Alex and I had been going on much the same as before I broke off with Ross. We dated now. We still spent a lot of time at his home or at the Conways', but in between we went out for such recreation as New Terra provides. On weekends we played tennis sometimes (that's more fun on Mars than on Earth because you can jump higher and send the ball three times as far). In the evening, there were occasional shows or concerts at the City Auditorium. Ballet in one-third gravity is like nothing you've ever imagined, if you've only seen it on Earth. The dancers leap unbelievably high and then float as if in a slow-motion movie. We went to the Star Tower to dance as well as to eat, and there were several restaurants that had live entertainment. Then, too, we went to parties at the homes of some of Alex's friends.

But the thing that I was expecting didn't happen; Alex never took me in his arms, never tried to kiss me, even. Of course I didn't really want him to. I dreaded it, in a way, because I knew it wouldn't be any good, it would only make my leaving more painful for us both. But you can't be sensible about a thing like that! I did want it. I did and I didn't at the same time. Everything in the way that Alex looked at me made me believe that he did, too; and yet now that I was free, the barrier between us seemed all the stronger for being invisible. Even when we danced he held me gingerly, as if I were his sister after all. *Oh, Alex,* I cried silently, *what is it that I'm doing—or not doing—that makes you think this is the way it still has to be? Or don't you love me at all? Perhaps I was imagining things before . . . but I really don't see how I could have been.*

This was not a situation I'd met before; with Ross, I had more often had the opposite problem. And harder to bear than my hurt feelings was the fact that I could see that Alex was not happy. He was remote, somehow, at the very moments we were closest. I began to wonder if he was caught up in some other sort of trouble, not related to me at all—something to do with his work, maybe? Alex never said much about his job and I knew he considered it merely a stepping-stone to things beyond, for there was talk of a new colony, to be called Syrtis City, in the planning stages.

One evening during the week before Alex and Alicia's group was to go to Phobos, when the Conway children were in bed and Kathy and I were alone in the living room watching TV, Kathy said to me, "Are you still homesick, Mel?"

I thought about it. "Not exactly homesick, I guess," I told her. "I still want to get back to Earth as soon as I can, but waiting isn't as hard as it was. I almost hope my reservation doesn't come through until the end of the term. I'm so involved with school right now, I'd hate to quit in the middle of a project. And besides, I'd lose the credit for the college courses I'm taking."

She smiled. "So New Terra isn't such a bad place to be?"

"Not for a while. Only—" I looked up and saw Paul coming in from the kitchen with the coffee things. It wasn't that I was shy with Paul; besides being a good friend, he was, after all, my pastor, and he'd been a tremendous help to me in coming to terms with Dad's death. But what I'd been about to say to Kathy wasn't a thing I could discuss with him.

I wondered how much Alex had said about me to Paul. The two were close friends as well as cousins.

"Only what?" Kathy prodded me.

I couldn't finish as I'd intended to, and so I burst out, to both of them, "Oh, there just isn't any solution to—to being torn in two!" Then I added, "Is there, Paul?" though I don't know what I wanted him to tell me.

Paul took it seriously, not as an idle comment. But he seemed at a loss. "I can't tell you what to do, Mel. I don't want to influence you, any more than a doctor wants his relatives for patients."

"I'm not a relative."

"No, but—" He stopped short, embarrassed. Suddenly I knew what he had started to say: *But Alex is—and this involves Alex!*

Kathy said, "Mel, have you ever given any serious thought to staying in the Colonies?"

"Permanently, you mean? I couldn't!"

"Why not?"

"Why—why I couldn't, that's all. I'm going to live at Maple Beach."

"In other words, you haven't opened your mind to the possibility."

"I've honestly tried to figure out how people can want to stay here."

"Always with that one premise, though—that as far as you're concerned, you've got to go back to Earth in order to be happy."

"But I do have to. I know it's hard for people here to understand, but it's just the way I am; I belong on Earth. I can't even imagine feeling any other way."

Kathy said thoughtfully, "Is the imagining really so impossible, Mel? How would you feel right now, for instance, if you had decided to stay here? Have you ever really pictured yourself as a Colonial and looked at things under that premise instead of the other one?"

"I guess I haven't. But I'm *not*—"

"Forget that. Pretend that you are—temporarily, to yourself, I mean."

"Is that what you mean by opening my mind to the possibility?"

"In a way. It might be an interesting thing to try."

"I know how to make it more interesting," Paul said suddenly.

"What's that?" I asked, intrigued.

"You aren't going to like this."

"I'd like to hear it, though."

"All right." Giving me a searching look, he began, "Suppose you were a Martian, a permanent resident of New Terra, without any of the particular problems you do have but with the same job and the same friends as you have now. What would you be doing this Saturday?"

"Saturday? Why, I suppose I'd—" Too late, I saw the trap. "Paul Conway, you're trying to get me to go on that ridiculous Phobos expedition."

He nodded calmly. "Guilty as charged."

"You and Alex are two of a kind! Why are you always trying to get me into things like that?"

"Maybe to solve the problem you say has no solution."

"You mean that if I go maybe I'll discover that I'm crazy about floating around in a pressure suit and forget all about Earth. It's not so simple."

"No, of course it's not." He hesitated. "This is going to be hard to explain. We could talk about it all night and still not cover it. But I'll try. Look, we're not a—a slice of Earth under glass here. Yet as long as you look at the Colonies that way, that's what you're going to see. A terrarium, a cage. You could live under these domes for fifty years and get used to all the 'incredible inconveniences,' as Janet put it, and you might convince yourself that it was okay; but it wouldn't be. You wouldn't be happy because it would still be a prison with bars."

"I know! That's exactly what I'm afraid of."

"No, it isn't," Kathy said gently. "You're afraid of what's outside the bars. The unknown. The bars are all in your own mind."

That was true, I thought suddenly. There were no bars for Paul and Kathy. There were none for Alex. There had been none for Dad.

Paul went on, "A Martian doesn't have quite the same outlook as a Terrestrial; he doesn't see Earth as a standard to measure by, he just takes Mars as it is." *And there's one particular Martian he's talking about,* I thought. "In order to understand, you've got to put yourself in a situation that's peculiarly Martian, only doing that isn't enough in itself. If you go into it with a 'grin and bear it' attitude, you won't learn anything except that you *can* grin and bear it, which you already know."

"That's like Janet's 'survive, maybe; but adapt, never!' theory," I reflected. "So far I've just pictured—surviving?"

"You're on the right track. If you made the sort of experiment Kathy was talking about, carried it through pretending that you were a Colonial—"

"Is that the reason Alex wants me to go to Phobos?" I asked directly. "The one he won't tell me?"

"Not quite. He's got something a little more specific in mind, nothing you need to worry about right now." Paul stood up. "End of sermon. I apologize; normally I try to avoid inflicting that sort of thing on my friends."

"But you've helped, Paul," I said warmly. "Thanks. I'll . . . think about it."

"I wish you would. Good night, Mel." He started toward the boys' bedroom, saying to Kathy, "I'll check on the kids before I turn in. Coming?"

As Kathy rose to join him, I stopped her. "Kathy? What if I do this and nothing changes? I mean, I really don't see how—"

"Why, then you'll know, won't you?" With some hesitation, she went on, "But if you do find out that it's an adjustment you can't make, then—then I think I would stop dating Alex, if I were you. You're making it very rough for him, you know."

"Am I?"

"You are. Darn it, I shouldn't say anything to you, but Alex is the closest thing Paul and I have to a brother, and we—well, frankly, Mel, we'd hate to see this dragged out any longer."

I stared at the floor. Somehow it hadn't occurred to me that the hopelessness of it all might be hurting Alex, too.

Paul paused in the doorway. Abruptly he said, "Mel, I'm going to break my own rule. There's something else I think you ought to know."

Kathy raised her eyebrows, but he shook his head at her and went on. "You mustn't ever let him know you've heard this, but Alex has been investigating job opportunities on Earth. Not seriously; he's just toying with the idea, so far—"

"Earth?" I said incredulously. "But that's crazy! Alex didn't like living on Earth, I know he didn't; everything he cares about and believes in is here. And even the gravity was hard on him. He'd be the very last person to go back." Alex, working on Earth? I thought. Alex commuting to one of those dismal metropolitan centers? Alex, a junior cog in one of those huge, impersonal companies? It wouldn't be only the triple weight that would drag him down. He'd be short of money for a long time after paying off his passage; it would be high even with his TPC discount, since he couldn't go as a student again. And if he ever did get enough together to start his own business, it would be just like thousands upon thousands of other businesses. No new cities to build, no unexplored lands—and as for any hope of getting into politics . . .

"You must be mistaken, Paul," I said. "Alex would be miserable on Earth. There'd be no challenge for him at all. Why, it would be worse than staying on Mars would be for me, even."

"I think so, too," he agreed.

"For goodness' sake, then, can't you stop him? Whatever would make him consider such a thing in the first place?"

"Haven't you guessed, Mel?" murmured Kathy.

I got the point. It was a possibility I hadn't even considered, and I knew that I couldn't consider it now. "All right," I said resolutely. "I'll go to Phobos. And if that doesn't change the way I feel, I'll move from here, and I—I won't see Alex again. Not at all, ever."

Chapter 14

It's funny how when you wake in the morning, you look forward to a day without having any idea at all of where that day will bring you. You may know what you're going to be doing, and you may have a fairly good picture of whether it will be pleasant or not; but you can't really imagine the outcome. For all you know, the day might hold the most glorious instant of your life or the thing that's your worst fear. That's a bit scary, if you think about it!

The day we went to Phobos was like that. I was trying not to look ahead at all. Early that morning, when Charlene woke me as she usually did with her gleeful three-year-old chatter, I pulled myself out of bed and dressed and brushed my hair, telling myself, *This is just an ordinary day. I live on Mars, and this is what it feels like!* But the day was not ordinary, and no amount of effort on my part could make it so. Sometimes you have to take things as they come.

I had consented to the trip not because I thought it could possibly change anything, but because it was a postponement of the time when I'd have to break off with Alex. Nevertheless, I was bound and determined to make it an honest test. Through-out the day I was truly going to pretend that I was staying on Mars, and not once was I going to console myself with the thought of Maple Beach. I was going to find out how it would feel, though I was very sure that it would be a feeling that I wouldn't like. I had been trying it out for the past few days. Kathy was right; that sort of mental adjustment gives you a whole new slant on things. But a new slant isn't enough, always. Perhaps it might be, if you could really maintain it when something rocks the boat—but you can't, of course.

The first part of the trip was uneventful. The shuttle we went in was an older, smaller model than those I'd encountered before, and carried no crew besides the pilot. Alex and I were the only adults along, since it was necessary to make room for as many eighth graders as possible. The kids were exuberant. We kept them in line with some assistance from Alicia, who had been elected class chairman for the occasion. During the flight we let them unstrap two at a time and taught them the rudiments of zero-g maneuvering; that was a full-time job that left me no chance to think about anything else.

I had some bad moments after we landed on Phobos, during the suiting-up process. A modern pressure suit isn't much like those bulky, restrictive ones used in the early days of space travel, and in fact it really isn't too uncomfortable, especially under low-g conditions. It has all the necessary conveniences, such as heating and cooling arrangements and a nippled water tank in case a person gets thirsty. But still, a spacesuit is a spacesuit, and its wearer is dependent on an air tank strapped to his back, which to me was the ultimate instrument for keeping me aware of the fact that the amount of air available was strictly limited.

"Didn't you ever do any scuba diving on Earth?" Alex asked me.

"No, and besides, that's different because you can always come to the surface," I argued. But with all those appraising eyes on me—you know how kids are!—I couldn't do anything but act as if putting on a spacesuit were a normal, everyday occurrence for me.

Alex and the pilot checked everyone's gear very carefully and saw to it that the helmets were adjusted properly and the suit radios were working before they opened up the ship. Those radios allowed everyone to hear all that anyone said, so there had to be some strict rules about obeying orders to keep quiet. (Since nobody wanted to be confined to the ship, we didn't have too much difficulty in enforcing them.) If you need to talk privately to anyone in a suit, you switch off your radio and simply touch helmets; Alex and I did that whenever we didn't want the kids to overhear.

Phobos is so close in that Mars fills half its sky; in crescent phase there's a huge red arc, one of the most fantastic sights I've ever seen. Full phase is even more spectacular. The kids were less interested in admiring the view than in jumping around, however, and we had to have a very strict rule about that. Everyone stayed hooked to a safety line—because it's possible to jump right off Phobos! It's actually been known to happen. The means of rescue, a rocket-powered scooter, was at hand; but our pilot wasn't at all anxious to use it.

The gravity on Phobos is so low that in effect it's zero; actually you weigh one thousandth of what you would on Earth, just enough to know where the ground is. I could, therefore, move much as I would have under zero-g, but I wasn't quite so disoriented. And the rocky terrain gave the illusion of being on a real planet because I didn't notice how close the horizon was, in spite of Phobos being only ten miles in diameter.

It was a strange new environment all right; yet somehow it didn't seem dreadful to me, except for the air tank business. Probably that was because I was so busy keeping track of the kids. As a matter of fact, though, I think my first impression was a kind of exhilaration. The funniest thing began to happen to me. Not only was it fun to float around under zero-g again, but along with the weight of Mars' gravity, another weight seemed missing, too: the weight of Earth. Of longing for Earth, I mean. I kept thinking, *I don't have to worry about that today. I can worry about it some other time, but today I am Martian, and I am free to enjoy this!*

But of course, my first impressions of Phobos are hard to sort out from the later ones.

The primary purpose of the shuttle trip had been to bring supplies to the Phobos research station. That station was merely a small pressurized hut in which two men could live for reasonably long periods, plus a collection of unpressurized storage sheds and weird-looking scientific equipment. The two scientists currently in residence came out to greet us when we arrived, and as we chatted the pilot handed them their mail, which included, as it happened, not only the usual discs of private e-mail, but a package from Earth. A package of any kind is an event to a Colonial, but a package of food is an unheard-of bonanza. And in this case it would have been better if it had remained unheard of.

I don't know what kind of food was in the package, but whatever it was, it was happily shared as soon as those two men got back to the hut and out of their suits. Thank heaven there wasn't room for us in there, so they could share it with us! Because whatever they ate was contaminated, and they were both deathly ill within the hour.

New Terrans aren't resistant to terrestrial bacteria; I suppose that may have had something to do with it. Ordinary shipments are carefully sterilized, but probably the health officials never thought any private individual would be crazy enough to invest offworld shipping charges in something edible. At any rate, the first thing I knew Alex was in a huddle with our pilot, their radios switched off and their helmets touching, and then they beckoned to me to join them and told me that if the two scientists didn't get to a hospital quickly, they might very well die.

Naturally, that meant starting back to Mars immediately. Alex and the pilot got the men into the ship while I broke the news to the youngsters. Before I got them aboard, though, Alex came back to me. He motioned for me to shut off my radio again and then we touched helmets so that we could talk privately. "Look, Mel," he said, "you know, don't you, that this ship can't carry extra passengers? That is, it could leave here under low-g, maybe, without having everyone strapped down in a seat, but it couldn't land safely."

"I guess it couldn't. But then what are we going to do, Alex? We've got to get those men back somehow."

"I know. So there's only one thing we can do. Are you going to be scared, Mel? Of being marooned here until the ship can get back again?"

"*Here?* On Phobos, alone?"

"Well, with me, of course. Does the idea frighten you?"

It was a stupid question; he must have known that just thinking about it made me sick. "Frankly, yes," I said in what I hoped was a fairly steady voice. "But there isn't anything else to do, is there? We certainly can't leave any of the kids."

"No. And since we can't leave the pilot, either, it's got to be you and me. You won't panic, will you? It will be quite a long wait. It takes time to refuel, besides nearly six hours for the round trip."

"Well, the research station people stay up here for weeks at a time." I was glad that the pressure suit hid the way I was shaking.

"Sure they do. It's not going to be bad, Mel. We'll be in radio contact with the ship and with Mars. Okay?"

"Okay." I wondered what would happen if it wasn't okay with me, because there was really no choice at all.

We got the kids rounded up, and while Alex had another talk with the pilot, I saw to it that they were strapped down in their seats. I hoped they weren't going to get too wild, left to themselves for the return trip, but most of them had been subdued by the presence of the two stricken men. Alicia took me aside, and as we touched helmets she said to me, "Don't worry, Mel. I'll take care of things."

"I'm sure you will, honey. Thanks."

She hugged me, then added confidentially, "Don't worry about yourself, either. Alex will take care of you."

"I'm sure of that, too." I *was* sure, I thought, and then I wondered, just when had I begun to depend so much on Alex? Just when had his presence started to make the difference between feeling safe and not feeling safe?

We went over to the hut and stood in its shadow while the ship lifted. A burst of fire blossomed out from under her, throwing heat and light out across the dead floor of gloomy little Phobos. For an instant she hovered, then the next thing I knew we were watching her stretch an incandescent wire across the sky and down toward the nearby horizon. The whole thing was utterly silent, like TV with the sound muted, but I could feel the vibration in the ground. I blinked; and when my eyes were wide open again, all I could see for a moment was a cluster of purplish jiggles between me and the stars.

Alex took my arm. "Lonely?" he asked straightforwardly.

"Yes. It's—eerie . . . all by ourselves out here." I looked back toward the deceptively warm-looking swollen arc of Mars. "And even there it's almost lifeless. All that desert—"

" 'They cannot scare me with their empty spaces,' " he quoted softly, " 'Between stars—on stars where no human race is—' "

"Robert Frost!" I took it up. " 'I have it in me so much nearer home, To scare myself with my own desert places.' Oh, Alex!

That's true—so true." With a sudden flash of understanding I burst out, "It's not really space that scares me, is it?"

"If you know that," Alex told me, "you've already taken a big step."

We turned to go into the hut. And that was where we met our first problem. We couldn't get in!

An airlock is not quite like an ordinary door. You don't just turn a knob and open it. It's a very complicated device that can't be made to work by just anyone. And besides that, all of them are a little different. Any astronaut could have figured this one out in short order, but Alex was not an astronaut; as a matter of fact, he had no technical training of any kind. He knew about pressure suits, having had previous experience with them, but he could not get the airlock to cycle properly. And naturally I was no help at all.

"This is about the stupidest thing I've ever pulled in my life," he admitted sheepishly, when it became apparent that it was hopeless. "I never thought about it. The pilot could have shown us, but I never thought to ask and he never thought that it wouldn't be obvious to me."

"Couldn't you talk to him on the radio," I suggested, "and ask him?"

"That's a nice idea," he agreed. "The only trouble is, the radio's in there. Our suit radios don't have the range—if they did, what we're saying to each other now wouldn't be private."

Forcing myself to stay calm, I asked, "What's going to happen to us, then?"

"Nothing bad, except that we're going to get hungry after a

while. These suits are good ones; we could stay in them a lot longer than we're going to have to. It's just an inconvenience, but I feel like a fool for putting you through it."

"How long will it take them to refuel?"

"A couple of hours, the pilot told me. They'll really push it, though, when they can't raise us on the radio."

We sat down—if what you do in almost zero-g can be called sitting—and looked ahead to a dismal eight-hour wait. I was silent, trying to quell a rising apprehension that I knew was illogical. Alex moved closer to me and put his suit-enclosed arm around my shoulders. "I should never have got you into this," he said.

"Nobody's infallible, Alex."

"I wasn't talking about the hut."

"Our having to stay here wasn't your fault. It was the only thing we could do. I'd have figured it out for myself in a few minutes."

"I didn't mean that, either. I—I'm sorry, Mel."

I tried to make a joke of it. "I'd have thought," I said mischievously, "that this would be just the sort of experience you'd think would be good for me! If I hadn't seen those sick men, I'd have suspected a put-up job."

He laughed. "Come on now, would I be as hard on you as all that?"

"I wouldn't put it past you. I really don't know why I trust you at all."

More soberly he said, "Maybe because I know you better than you know yourself."

"Alex—will you tell me your real reason for getting me to come along on this little jaunt?"

"Someday, maybe. This isn't the time or the place. This last part wasn't intended; you do know that, don't you? The best-laid plans can backfire."

"I know. I was kidding, Alex."

"Well anyway," he decided, "here. we are, and since we're stuck we may as well relax—"

"And enjoy it?" I finished, somewhat bitterly, though I was trying to smile. "Like zero-g?"

"Like zero-g." His voice was warm, remembering. "Seriously, though, Mel, it will be pleasanter if we do relax. We aren't in any danger, you know."

"I guess you think I'm an awful coward."

I could hear his quick breath of surprise. "Of course I don't. I think you have more courage than most people have."

"Me? You sure haven't been very observant, then." I sighed. "I only wish you were right."

"Don't you know you're courageous, Mel?" He turned to me, though with the suit radios it didn't make the slightest difference how we were facing. "Maybe you don't, but I've seen you do one thing after another that proves it. For instance, there are a lot of Terrestrials who would have become pretty hysterical watching that ship take off the way we just did."

"Well, I was scared stiff. I still am. But I'm just not the hysterical type, that's all."

"No. You're not; the way you reacted to your dad's death showed that. And there have been some other things. There's a whole string of them that I could name. You've got plenty of courage but you don't know how to use it to your own advantage. You can bear up under anything that's thrown at you, yet you won't let go—you won't reach out."

"How do you mean, reach out? What should I reach for?"

"Anything you want, even if you're not sure what it is. Don't stick to what you've got just because it's there and you're comfortable with it. Some people have to; that's the only safe way for them. But not you, Mel! You don't have to wonder whether you can cope, you know you can. Because you *do* it. It's the best security anybody can have."

Anything I want, I reflected. *But oh, Alex, there are two things I want now, and I can't have both! Maybe I can't have either one.*

Suppose, just suppose I should forget about all the plans, all the safe, happy years at Maple Beach, and decide I'm willing to spend the rest of my life on that outlandish, alien planet off there—would I have your love? Paul and Kathy think so, but they could be mistaken. They must be, for in all this time you've never so much as kissed me! Good Lord, Alex, we're not children. Even if we were years younger, a date would at least end in a good-night kiss, and we'd be beyond that stage now, wouldn't we, if we really loved each other? That's one way customs can't differ on Mars!

On the other hand, suppose I never see you again. Will Maple Beach be a safe, happy place . . . or will it be just as much of a cage as these tightly sealed domes seem to be? Will I simply have found myself a new prison?

"Do you reach out for what you want?" I asked, with a kind of shyness I hadn't felt before.

"Usually."

"But not always?"

"Not when I might get it, and—and mess up somebody else's life." His voice was low.

All at once it struck me what he was talking about. *How imperceptive I've been!* I thought. *We're not children, and we're not playing children's games. What might happen between us wouldn't be a casual thing, as it is between a man and woman who don't care for each other in any other way. It wouldn't ever be, so Alex won't start that. Not because he wouldn't get anywhere, but because he* would. *He knows it and I know it. If he were to express love for me in the— the usual way, I would marry him. I've been roped into a lot of things less easily than I'd be roped into that! I would push all my other feelings out of the way and marry him; but we wouldn't live happily ever after. As soon as the newness, the thrill, wore off, one of two things would happen. Either we'd break up and I'd go back to Maple Beach for a divorce, or I'd stay on Mars and resign myself to being miserable. The captive in the terrarium. He doesn't want that, and he knows that if we were once to start, we wouldn't be able to stop.*

So there we were. I sat there with Alex and looked off at the huge, sky-filling globe that was Mars, and little by little my nerves calmed a bit and I got back to where I could go on trying to imagine that as home, and I realized that the things I'd been thinking about most, recently, were all *there,* not at Maple Beach at all! And still, I couldn't change myself. I couldn't make the choice; it was, I supposed, already made, as so many choices are. Earth was too much a part of me. There would never be a moment when I could bring myself to say, irrevocably, "Earth no longer matters." It is not the sort of decision that you reach out for; it's got to be forced on you. Alex could force it, but he would not. Some people never adapt, and he would not take that risk— so maybe I would never know. Maybe I would always wonder, back at Maple Beach, if I was there because I really wanted to be or only because it was easiest to let things ride.

Alex and I spent most of those hours on Phobos just talking; there wasn't much else to do aside from throwing rocks off into space, and though a world where what goes up doesn't come down may be fascinating to start with, the novelty quickly wears off. The only thing we really had to do was to switch air tanks at the proper intervals. That was not a process I enjoyed, although it was simple enough, for it gave me the shivers. I didn't even like to look at the little gauge that told when it was time.

It's possible to change your own tank but it's much easier to do each other's, and that was the way we went at it. Alex told me exactly what to do—there are some clamps to be dealt with and valves to be turned in the proper sequence—but my fingers were trembling so that on the first try I dropped the fresh cylinder with the main outlet valve open. It shook me so much that I just stood there stupidly and watched the thing shoot off like a rocket, with the air hissing away into space.

A pressure suit holds enough air for you to have a little lee-way, and if Alex was upset, he didn't let me see it. "Take it easy, Mel," he said quietly. "Get another one—no, you can't salvage that. It can't be helped now."

"Couldn't you do it?" I asked helplessly.

"Yes, if I need to, but you may as well learn. Just take it slow and steady this time. There's no need to hurry."

I managed it all right, and at the next change every thing went okay. There was a loosely secured pile of the tanks near the hut where we were sitting, on which I kept a wary eye; but I managed to push it out of my mind for several hours. By that time, though, I was getting a little headache from being hungry—it had been a long time since breakfast—and slightly dizzy, either from that or just from being where I was. We had run out of things to talk about. I stared at those air tanks, thinking of how they were the very last thing I'd ever wanted to have anything to do with, and then idly I began to count them.

There were not enough.

I knew how often we'd been switching them; I knew that they were all the same size; and I was perfectly able to do simple arithmetic. There were not quite enough to last until that shuttle could get back to us, figuring its arrival on the most optimistic basis; there wouldn't have been even if I hadn't wasted one.

Having almost enough air is not one bit better than having no air. It doesn't make a great deal of difference whether or not you almost make it if, in the final analysis, you don't. You can't stretch air the way people lost in a desert can ration water. Neither can you talk to a spaceship on your radio—assuming that you've got access to a radio—and tell it to please hurry up. It can't get where it's going any faster than it can, no matter how great the urgency. The laws that govern survival in space are inexorable; and unrealistic as I may have been in some of my feelings, I was practical enough to know that.

My first reaction to knowing it was a kind of paralysis, out of which emerged two thoughts: first, *this can't be happening!* and second, *why didn't Alex tell me?*

He must have known as soon as he found that we couldn't get into the hut. Through all that cheerful banter, all those calm reassurances, he must have known! Why hadn't he told me the truth? Well, it was all too obvious why he hadn't; there would be nothing to gain by it and a great deal to lose. Alex knew how I felt about air. We hadn't discussed it specifically, but of course he'd known for a long time. In this situation anyone would feel terror; but my terror would be worse, and he would spare me for as long as he could. How long was that going to be?

The arithmetic told me. Then—and this was the really horrible part—I began to do another kind of arithmetic. And the answer was that I would never be allowed to run out of air at all, Alex being what he was.

I thought back to the very first time I'd been frightened by the concept of airlessness, in the *Susie,* and I remembered the thing Janet had said that triggered it. *Do you know what would happen if a spaceship ran low on air? They'd draw lots . . . because the air would last twice as long for half as many people, of course.*

But Alex would not draw lots. He would make his own decision, and I had no real doubt as to how he would make it. He would not consult me. It would be carried out in some way that would keep me from knowing anything about it until it was too late to protest.

I'd thought I'd known what it was to be afraid—but I hadn't, not until then. The terror you feel for a person you love is much, much worse than the fear you feel for yourself. And if there had been any doubt before about my loving Alex, there was none at that moment. There was no room in me for any thought but one: *There's got to be a way . . . please, God, there must be a way to save Alex! Somehow, someway, I've got to find it; no matter what I have to do or how I have to do it, that's the only thing I care about!*

The whole thing took place within a few instants; Alex looked at me, and even through my helmet he could see that something was up. "Mel, what's the matter?" he demanded. "You're not going to get sick, are you—"

"I'm all right," I whispered, my lips dry.

He came over to me and clutched my arm. "Don't hold out on me," he said curtly. "If there's anything wrong, I've got to know it."

"Then don't you hold out on me!"

"What does that mean, for Pete's sake?"

"Alex," I said shakily, "I can count as well as you can." I glanced meaningfully at the small stack of cylinders.

"Air tanks? But there are more, in one of those storage sheds; it was just restocked with the supplies we brought. These are just the extras we had out for the kids. Good Lord, Mel, surely you didn't think I'd cut it that close! This wouldn't have given us any reserve at all." He made a more careful survey. "Why, there aren't even *enough* here."

"I—I noticed that."

"Noticed it? How do you mean?" He chuckled. "Sure, you've got a kind of fixation on the subject of canned air, but you must have known that I wouldn't let anything happen to you."

"I knew that, Alex."

"Then you didn't really think you were going to run short at the end, did you?" He started to laugh, then got a better look at my face. Gripping my arm he said urgently, "Did you, Mel?"

"No," I said in a very low voice. "No—I thought you were." I moved toward him, my first stunned relief expanding into joy. "Oh, Alex! I—I didn't know before what loving someone means."

He didn't answer. He just held me close—as close as he could considering those clumsy pressure suits—and without words we both knew that there was nothing to worry about at all, anymore.

After a few minutes he said to me, "It's all right now, isn't it?" And I knew he didn't mean just this particular scare.

"Everything's all right," I whispered, feeling a kind of awe that I could know so much happiness at such a time, in such an unearthly place.

We laughed, then. We agreed on the silliness of my having been so obsessed with my own special fears that I fell right into believing the very worst, without any justification at all. Because, all of a sudden, even I could feel that it *had* been silly— senseless, neurotic, anything you want to call it. Ever since the beginning it had been. That sort of fruitless phobia carries its own penalty; I'd gotten exactly what I was looking for, and I had brought it on myself.

But things weren't quite as simple as that. All the time we

were talking about it, underneath I was thinking that foolish as my assuming the worst had been, it had happened. And when it happened, something else had, too. For a moment I had actually believed that there was not enough air. And I hadn't reacted at all the way I'd have thought I would! I hadn't panicked as far as I myself was concerned. The only thought in my mind during that moment had been *Alex*. Better that this thing should happen to me than to him, better even that it should happen to both of us than for me to live without Alex! And if I felt that way then, how could I ever have imagined that I could leave Alex just for Earth?

Would it have happened that way without all that melodramatic business? Would just going to Phobos have accomplished anything by itself, as Paul had thought it might? I don't know; I only know that that silly phobia of mine wasn't a total waste of energy, because through it I found out something. I found out that my love for Alex is the most significant thing in any world for me—and now, I don't see how I could once have thought otherwise.

Chapter 15

I never wanted to come to Mars, but here I am, and I'm here to stay. I still miss Maple Beach; I always will. But there's a hill out near where Syrtis City is going to be that's shaped almost like the one that rises back of Gran's house, and from a photograph of it Kathy helped me to make a "window" like hers. I can see it from the table where I often sit to study, and you know, it's rather beautiful, really.

Alex and I were married on the fifty-sixth of November. If life were like what's shown in movies, I suppose we would have fallen into each other's arms there on Phobos—spacesuits or no spacesuits!—and that would have been that, with everything all settled. It didn't happen quite that way. Would you really want to become engaged while wearing a pressure suit and helmet? Also I think Alex felt that I had had enough excitement for one afternoon, which was very probably true. So we just went on talking as if nothing had happened. Then when the ship got there, all kinds of people were with it, even a doctor, for everyone had been absolutely frantic at our not answering them on the radio. During the return flight we got those miserable suits off and enjoyed a long-delayed meal, but we didn't have any privacy.

We weren't alone again until we got back to the Conways'. Then, before we went in, Alex did kiss me . . . and it was worth waiting for.

He told me that he had loved me ever since those days aboard *Susie*, only at first he couldn't do anything about it because I was tied up with Ross; and then later he couldn't because we had grown too close for casual kisses and, as I had guessed, he was unwilling to pressure me into anything that I would regret in the future. "You do understand, don't you, Mel?" he said. "I didn't want one of those temporary things! Not with you. With you it had to be for the rest of our lives—or nothing. Because I couldn't let you be hurt."

I understood. The difference between real love and the thing that often goes by that name is as great as the difference between imagining a place and being there. That will always be true, on this planet or on any other.

We delayed the wedding a whole Martian month, fifty-six interminable days, which was undoubtedly a wise thing to do because my change of heart had been rather sudden; but I'm afraid we didn't have any such sensible motivation as that. We simply couldn't get an apartment any sooner. (And we wouldn't have gotten this one, except through a personal friend of Paul's.) Alex kidded about taking me Outside for a honeymoon, but that wouldn't have been very practical; there's no place to stay out there!

You might think that I'd be more bothered by the fact of the Martian atmosphere being unbreathable than ever, after that harrowing experience. Well, strangely enough it seems to have worked the other way. Partly, I guess, I've got a feeling that the worst is already over; and that's just as irrational as the other feeling, although it may have something to do with what Alex said about knowing you can cope. I'm certain, though, that nothing in the future can be as bad as those few moments on Phobos. And that's very fortunate indeed. Because I found out why Alex and Paul were so anxious to get me to Phobos in the first place. They were both sure that I was more adaptable than I thought I was, and for anyone who's going to marry a person with the plans Alex has, this pressure suit business is a good thing to adapt to! It seems that if you're in on the founding of a new colony, there aren't any domes at first.

When I went to get my Colonial entry visa converted into a permanent immigration permit, I was a bit nervous. I remembered Dr. Spencer, the psychiatrist who'd given me my medical certificate back on Earth, and that he'd said, *If I were interviewing you for an emigration permit, I wouldn't approve it.* Surely there wouldn't be any trouble over that! If I married Alex, they'd have to accept me, wouldn't they? Then I thought of something else Dr. Spencer had said: *You could surprise yourself.* And he'd been right. How had he known? When I'd been so sure that my ideas would never change, how had he known that it wasn't the permanent sort of sureness? I'd grown up since then, I realized. I had become truly sure, and for that reason they would let me stay.

Two weeks before the wedding, I was unexpectedly notified by TPC that because of a last-minute cancellation there was a cabin for me on the S.S. *Fortune,* which was in port at the time. "Are you positive that you don't want to take it?" Alex asked me.

"Absolutely positive," I declared, laughing.

He made me face him. "Mel," he said, "I'm going to tell you something that I think you already know, but I've got to be very sure you know it. If you cancel this reservation, there will never be another chance to go back on your return trip ticket. That ticket will be forfeit, and its value credited to your dad's firm. You're aware of how much those tickets cost, aren't you? Besides, you'll lose your place on the waiting list, which is about three years long right now—"

"I know what it means, Alex. It means I'll never see Earth again."

"Never's a long time. Have you really thought about what you'll be losing?"

I wasn't anxious to go through the process a second time, but that's the way Alex is; he doesn't let me shy away from things. And he knew what he was doing. I'd been pushing all sorts of thoughts way back into my mind for weeks, ever since I'd decided to stay. Little things, memories like the clean, wet touch of rain, the warmth of the noonday sun, the fresh scent of terrestrial spring—and the glorious freeness of being able to walk, unprotected, under an open sky with a vast sea of air all around. Alex knew that if I was going to shed any tears over these, this was the best time for it. We talked for a long time that evening, and though I did cry near the end, there won't be any ghosts of Earth around to haunt me, now; at least not any that I have to hide from.

Afterward Alex said to me, "Am I forgiven, darling? You see why I did that, don't you?"

"I think so. Shutting out reality—telling yourself that a thing isn't going to hurt when it is—is just asking for trouble, right?"

He held me close to him. "Switching planets isn't as simple as moving from one country to another; I know! Don't ever think that I don't know."

"I won't," I said happily. "But details like whether we live on Earth or on Mars aren't as important as you think they are. The unchanging, *real* things are in people's hearts."

He laughed and squeezed his arms tight around me. "That's what I've been trying to convince you of all along!"

Our wedding day was everything I could have hoped for. Paul married us, naturally, and Kathy was matron of honor. Alicia was a junior bridesmaid, though we didn't have a large wedding party, and there were none of the fancy trimmings girls expect on Earth. I couldn't have a long wedding gown; but I did have a white dress, made over from one of Ms. Preston's, and I wore Mother's silver beads with it. (White's practical for everyday here, with our dustless, filtered air, so it's a very welcome addition to my small wardrobe.) And I had a magnificent bouquet, picked from the Champs-Elysées gardens with the special blessings of the city council.

We chose a traditional form of the service, a particularly lovely one, I think—the one where the bride says *whither thou goest I will go, and whither thou lodgest I will lodge* during the exchange of rings. Isn't it strange, how words from so long ago and so far away can still be so appropriate?

We're going to the new colony of Syrtis City when the time

comes; it'll be a few years yet before it's founded, but Alex is on the planning committee. What's more, he wants to go before the first dome is up. It'll be hard—dangerous, even. We won't have the comforts New Terra provides. During the early stages we'll be living in a pressurized hut and going Outside every day. (We'll both have to learn how to cycle the airlock!) I don't like the idea, especially considering the baby there'll be before then, but I guess if another city is to be built, that's the way it's got to start.

Meanwhile, besides going to college, I'm still working at the school part-time. I'll probably transfer to the high school as soon as I qualify for my teaching credentials. From the career stand-point, I'm better off here than I'd ever have been at Maple Beach; teachers have higher status in the Colonies than on Earth. And now that I see things objectively, I know my career does matter to me. (The Maple Beach school wasn't a very good one—that was why Dad and Gran sent me away to school—yet I'd planned to teach there indefinitely! It never even occurred to me that I'd have to move if I wanted a promotion.) I'm fortunate; I wasn't faced with a really hard choice about marriage, a choice between my work and living with the person I love. It's ironic. Julie Tamura wrote that she was surprised to hear I'd given up "every-thing" to become a homesteader's wife, which goes to show how little some people know about the Colonies.

Of course I don't care about advancement for the sake of salary, since on top of our earnings and Alex's secondary home-stead rights, we have what I inherited from Dad plus all that in-surance money. But I'd like to take part in establishing the new colony's schools. Besides, we're going to put all of Dad's money into the Syrtis City venture. That's what will get it on its feet, Alex believes—using locally controlled funds instead of depending on subsidies from Earth's governments. So you might say that Dad accomplished something for Mars after all, and I know that would please him.

Alex and I have rather a full social life, and not only with our own friends, because occasionally we're invited to the sort of function I used to attend with Dad. I'm learning not to hate it, because I know I'm going to be in for a lot more of that kind of thing if Alex's ambitions work out the way I think they will. It's lucky I had some experience and got well acquainted with people like the Ortegas. If and when Alex decides to run for some sort of office, I want to be a help, not a hindrance, though I doubt if I'll decide to go into politics myself.

Around the first of January, when the *Oregon Trail* came in again, I had a happy surprise: a wedding present from Gran! I'd never dreamed that she would send anything; she can't afford interplanetary shipping rates any better than most people can. But this wasn't a package, it was simply a fairly thick envelope. At first I was puzzled, because Gran and I correspond regularly through the normal data-link channel; there'd be no reason to send a letter aboard a ship, for it would be out-of-date weeks before it got here.

But the envelope didn't contain a letter, other than a brief handwritten note. Its bulk came from something wrapped in white tissue and sealed with gilt-edged tape. It was the locket! My ancestor Melinda Stillwell's gold locket, that had traveled the long, hard ox trail across terrestrial plains and mountains, all those many years ago.

I could imagine Gran standing by the window as she wrapped it, looking out at the shimmering blue ocean that I shall never see again. Holding the locket up and swinging it by its chain as I used to do when I was little, I thought of how I'd once wished that I'd been a pioneer woman in an unsettled land. Never make a wish unless you're prepared to see it come true in some astonishing way that you'd never even dream of! Because that may be how it turns out, though if you're lucky, like me, you'll also get some things that you didn't have the sense to wish for.

Now, strange as it still seems to me, I'm truly beginning to think of myself as a Martian! Is there anything more to it than love? Do I believe in the big dream myself, at all?

Well, I've pondered it a lot, and this is what I think: It's the future. Because if you don't believe that human beings will keep growing and changing and moving on, you don't believe in the future at all. If Alex and I weren't here, there'd be others; that's how it's always been, all the way from ancient times through the New World colonies, the western pioneers, the colonization of this solar system—and someday on to the stars. It may be Manifest Destiny as Alex says, or it may simply be that people, individual people, always want to see what's over the hill. It may be something else. But I do believe that if this thing wasn't being done by *somebody*, Earth would be in real trouble someday. I know enough now to say that you can't put permanent bounds on your horizons.

Things never stay the same, and that goes for worlds, too. You can't impose stability on the human race any more than on your own life. A civilization that can't expand will turn to violence, I'm told. Or at least decay. How paradoxical that the only way to assure the future for Earth is to leave it!

Maybe it's not what I'd have chosen to do alone. In fact I'm fairly sure it's not, but Alex wants it, and I love him. After all, that first Melinda wouldn't have chosen the covered wagon journey, either, if not for love of her husband, Jess. Maybe she lay in the bare, drafty log cabin night after night dreaming of the old Massachusetts seaport town, the way I dream of Maple Beach. The way the pilgrims who built that town must have dreamed of England. . . .

If the baby's a boy, we're going to name him after Dad. If it's a girl, I think we'll name her Susan—maybe even Susan Constance—because, while not all our memories of *Susie* are happy ones, it was in those days that we began to fall in love. And the very name *Susan Constant* was always something of a symbol for us.

Perhaps when little Susan gets old enough, she'll enjoy playing with Gran's locket, the way I used to do, and perhaps someday she'll have a daughter of her own to pass it on to. I wonder how many times it will be handed down before it comes to the girl who'll look wistfully back at a faint star, growing still dimmer in the center of a viewport, and say: "That's the sun." Not Earth, or Mars, but the sun! There will always be new worlds, I guess, as long as there are new generations.

Afterword to the 2006 Edition

This story, first published in 1970, was written several years earlier—before the Apollo flights to the moon, before anyone had gone to another world in a spaceship and looked back at Earth from a distance. It was based on the ideas I had about space when I myself was growing up. Yet when I came to revise it for republication, I found that the only facts to be updated, apart from the details of references to computer technology, were those related to the discoveries made in 1976 by the Viking landings on Mars.

In most ways, the story's initial edition was more relevant to today's world than to the era during which I wrote it—and there are more young people today who share my interest in the future. But I have made some minor changes that reflect modern women's outlook toward marriage and toward careers. My views of these things have changed more than my views of space have. I believe more than ever in all that I originally said about the significance of space colonization.

The settlement of new worlds may not proceed just as I've described it. Like many space advocates, I now think that the problems of Earth such as overpopulation and pollution can best be solved by building human habitats not on distant planets, but in space itself. It's possible that orbiting colonies will become a reality before Martian colonies do, although this book does not mention them. That makes no real difference to the story. Society a century from now will not be just as it's imagined today in any case; still people's dreams and people's feelings will remain the same.

Readers who would like to talk about the story are invited to write to me at sle@sylviaengdahl.com, and to visit my Web site at http://www.sylviaengdahl.com. I'm looking forward to meeting you there.